Mahn

D1123976

Worlds Apart

Worlds Apart

I have lived on the lip
of insanity, wanting to know reasons,
knocking on a door. It opens.
I've been knocking from the inside!

— Jelaluddin Rumi (1207–1273),
  Sufi mystic and poet, born
  in what is now Afghanistan

Translated by Coleman Barks with John Moyne,
in *The Enlightened Heart: An Anthology of Sacred Poetry*,
ed. Stephen Mitchell (New York: Harper & Row, 1989)

Worlds Apart

1

Did you ever have one of those days when you had to pack up and leave your regular life behind? Say goodbye to your friends, your school, your neighborhood, and start someplace else?

Did you ever have one of those days when your nice, normal life got thrown out with the trash? And you found you were leaving town to *make a fresh start,* with strict orders to *keep family matters private,* and your new *home* was a mental institution?

Did you ever have one of those days?

Neither had I. Until today, November 1, 1959.

Until today, we lived in a nice, normal Chicago neighborhood. My parents seemed pretty much like everybody else's parents. Every day Dad went to his office in the medical building downtown. *Maxwell May, M.D.* read the sign on the frosted glass of his office door. Mom spent her time with her friends, playing bridge and doing volunteer stuff with the hospital auxiliary. At least once a week we'd have dinner at the country club. I'd meet my friends there and go swimming or play tennis.

A couple of months ago I started my eighth year at Morningside Academy. I belonged to the French Club—*très chic*—and played violin in the orchestra. Best of all, I was a Starling. That was the name of our group. No one outside the group was supposed to know, but it stood for "darling little stars." That's what our dean of student life always said the young ladies of Morningside Academy should strive to be in this dark world—darling little stars.

As eighth graders, if our grades were good enough, we were allowed to start going to the Saturday afternoon sock-hops at the upper school. I'd been practicing dance steps all summer with the other Starlings. When we weren't doing the mashed potato or the twist, we were trying on outfits from each other's closets and picking out the perfect coordinating shade of lipstick.

Then one day, one innocent Tuesday, my parents were waiting for me in the kitchen when I got home from school. Right away I sensed an ambush.

Dad was pacing, holding on to an orange so tightly that I expected it to turn into a handful of pulp before he was through with it. Mom was sitting in the breakfast nook looking like she'd just been slapped in the face with a dead fish.

"Big news," they told me.

A puppy? A trampoline? A new baby?

"We're moving," Dad said.

My turn for the dead fish. "Moving? To a new house? When?"

"We're moving to Minnesota," Dad said. "Immediately."

"But—why?"

My parents exchanged the look—the one that says they don't want me to know what's going on. Dad turned away first, suddenly busy at the sink peeling the orange he'd finished strangling.

Mom took a deep breath. She spread her hands out on the table and appeared to be studying her firecracker-red fingernails.

"Your father has to leave his medical practice because of the x-ray burns on his hands. He can't scrub for surgery anymore, so he's taken a position at an ... institution—a special hospital where he won't be required to operate."

I knew Dad had some trouble with a few lingering sores on the knuckles of one hand, but this didn't make sense. "Dad, what's going on? Your hands—"

"Winnie, I don't—it's not—" he said.

"Max! It's true enough!" my mother said.

And that was the end of it.

2

On the long, silent road from Chicago to the Middle of Nowhere, I sit between my parents in the front seat of our overloaded car.

Usually I'm wild about family car trips. Even though I complain ahead of time about having to leave my friends behind for a week or two, once we're on the road I love the feeling of being in our own little world. I stretch out in the backseat with a new Nancy Drew. Dutiful Dad is at the wheel, interrupting his own whistling every five minutes to point out the sights or to read the latest Burma-Shave signs. (*Substitutes/Will let you down/Quicker/Than a/Strapless gown!*) Mom, who normally acts like it's her job to hold the universe together, is relaxing for a change, head back and humming along with the radio, usually Billie Holiday until the Chicago jazz station fades out.

Then we might play Name That Tune, or Dad's version of Twenty Questions—"Guess Which Bone of the Body I'm Thinking of and Spell It." Every now and then Mom dispenses road snacks from the picnic basket at her feet. Carrot sticks, apple slices, and Chex mix, each packed in its own container from the last Tupperware party she went to, plus Kool-Aid and coffee from matching plaid Thermos bottles.

We've traveled all the way to the Grand Canyon like this. To the Everglades. Niagara Falls.

I always have my camera with me, a bright red Brownie Starflash. On vacation I can shoot as many rolls of film as I want. I write notes about every picture I take so I'll know how to iden- tify it in my photo album. Sometimes I stalk around my subjects, framing shot after shot, imagining what it would be like to be on assignment for *Life* or *National Geographic*. Or sometimes I lie flat on my back and take pictures of the underside of a picnic table.

At home I try not to be so obvious about taking photos. The other Starlings tease me about looking like some dorky tourist carrying a camera everyplace, although they don't complain about all the neat pictures I take of them.

On vacation I don't have to make excuses about looking at the world through the eye of my Starflash. It's amazing how people— even strangers—will let you stare at them as long as you have that little box in front of your face. When people pose for a picture, they think they're in control of what you're seeing. But the camera always picks up something more.

It may be true that every picture tells a story, but it's not the whole story. It may not even be the true story.

But this isn't a day I want to capture on film. It's moving day, leaving-and-never-going-back day. Dad isn't whistling. Mom isn't humming. Billie Holiday is dead. So is my life.

After nearly eight hours on the road, most of it in heavy rain and fog, I'm ready to burst out of my skin. When we cross the Mississippi River, we leave behind the winding roads and hilly countryside of Wisconsin (*Don't/Try passing/On a slope/Unless you have/A periscope!*) for flat Minnesota farmland (*Said Farmer Brown/Who's bald/On top/ Wish I could/Rotate the crop!*) and town after boring little town.

At last, beyond the slap-slapping of the windshield wipers, there's a sign: *Bridgewater. Population 1,253.* We pass a two-block stretch of stores, a couple of cafés, two churches, and a gas station. The entire downtown slips by the windows of our car in a watery blur. On the other side of town we cross a narrow bridge that takes us over the rushing brown water of the Rye River. I see a tall fence topped with barbed wire running alongside the road.

We turn in at a gated entrance where another sign announces that we've arrived at the Bridgewater State School and Hospital. A security guard approaches the car. Dad introduces himself and shows some papers. Everything takes so long! Will we ever be out of this stuffy car? Finally the guard hands over a set of keys.

"Drive right up past the administration building, Dr. May. The road bends to the left for a piece. Your house is just around the corner. Can't miss it. It's the only one."

"The only one!" I tug at Dad's sleeve and lean toward the guard's face in the open window. "What about the other doctors' families? I thought—"

"Shh!" Mom puts a hand on my knee. "Not now."

Already Dad has cranked his window shut and the guard is waving us on. I twist around in the seat. Between the boxes stacked in the back window I catch a glimpse of the gate closing behind us.

Mom lets out a shivery sigh. "If anyone wanted to escape this place, they'd have to sprout wings and fly."

3

On our first night in the new house I can't remember how to fall asleep. Boxes are stacked everywhere. Moonlight slices in around the sheets hung at the windows as temporary curtains, throwing odd shadows around the room. The furniture isn't arranged right. Nothing fits.

And it's so quiet! I strain my ears at the silence, but it only seems deeper against the high-pitched crooning of crickets and frogs. Who knows what else might be lurking in the woods around here and along the river. This much quiet is too much. It's eerie.

The only traffic I hear is a patrol car cruising by at six minutes past the hour, every hour. Each time the headlights' glow crawls across the bare walls of my room, I feel like someone is searching for me with a flashlight. I hide deeper under the covers.

Finally the thick shade of night thins to fuzzy predawn gauze and I slide into a ragged patch of dreams …

"I was riding on a little sailboat," I tell Dad later in the kitchen. "But the boat kept getting smaller and skinnier, like a surfboard. I was trying to get back to shore, because the bay was crowded with enormous ships. And the waves were huge!"

"It's good you know how to swim," Dad says.

"Da-ad ..."

"I bet you didn't do much dreaming after the whistle blew this morning at six. Are you almost ready?"

"No, Dad. Listen! This was so real! My little boat had shrunk to the size of a water ski, and I was trying to ride through those waves. I was afraid I was going to be sucked down under those big ships. Something about them seemed evil, like they were out to get me or—"

"Where the devil *is* everything!"

I jump at the sound of Mom's voice behind me as she storms into the room.

"I swear, Max," Mom says, rummaging through a box on the kitchen counter, "those moving men you hired had the brains of earthworms! Half our things must have been left behind!" For dramatic effect she starts slamming everything that's slammable. "Has anybody seen the damn tea bags?"

My mother's temper tantrums give me the giggles. I chew on a lock of my hair to hide my amusement, but it doesn't fool her. She glares at me.

"Ladies," Dad says, beginning to jingle the coins in his pocket, "we really have to go. Now."

"Just let me finish telling my dream!" I yelp.

"Tell us on the way," Dad says, practically pushing Mom and me out of the kitchen. As he swings open the front door, I hear Mom pull in a sharp breath, as if she needs to take in enough air to swim across the ocean.

My mind flashes back to my dream. A towering wave rose above me on the shrinking board, and I felt the grip of powerful hands at my waist. *Don't fight it,* a voice instructed my dreaming self. *Take a deep breath, and remember—*

That's when I was ripped out of those strong hands by the scream of the six o'clock siren. Out of my dream. Plunged into this strange new world.

4

The three of us climb the wide steps of the red-brick administration building to a veranda supported by white columns. The door is locked for security purposes, a sign tells us, so Dad rings the bell.

This main building is flanked on either side by slightly smaller versions of itself. Dad gestures broadly and forces a smile. "It looks like a college campus, doesn't it?"

College? Who's he trying to fool? There are bars on the windows!

A buzzer sounds and the door opens. The chief administrator, Dr. Bonner, is here, shaking hands all around. He pulls us into a poorly lit room off the main lobby, where a group of other doctors have gathered to greet us—the newcomers.

The names go by too fast. There's a lady doctor from India dressed in a sari. Another lady doctor speaks in an accent that reminds me of the Russian woman who served piroshkis at a little tearoom back home. The dentist has terrible breath. There's a tall, wobbly doctor who appears to have a bad leg, but when he speaks, I realize he's drunk.

"On behalf of my colleagues," Dr. Bonner says, "welcome to all of you! I can't tell you how pleased we are to have you here."

Coffee and orange juice are offered, along with a tray of little round things that could be puffy cookies or flat muffins.

Dr. Bonner carries on. "Anything we can do to help you settle in, Mrs. May, I hope you'll let me know. And you, too, Winifred. All righty?"

"It's Winona," I tell him.

"Hmmm? What's that?" Dr. Bonner squints at me as if I'm some annoying bug.

"Our daughter's name is Winona," Mom explains. She's used to doing this when people first encounter my name. "Not Winifred."

"A simple mistake," Dad says, looking eager to please. "It's not a common name."

"Oh, it's not unheard of around here," Dr. Bonner replies. "We have several in our population."

I don't like the idea of having anything in common with Dr. Bonner's population. "It's Winnie, for short."

Dr. Bonner tosses an abrupt nod and a wink in my direction.

I bite my lip. Winkers make me want to scream! There aren't any right words to say to them. I never know if they expect me to wink back—something I would absolutely refuse to do even if I knew how to wink.

The other doctors begin to drift away, and Dr. Bonner claps Dad on the back. "You and I will get down to business soon enough. For now, I don't want to tax the ladies' patience, so let me take you all on a cook's tour of our facility. Just the highlights. I think you'll be impressed with the infirmary, the lab, and the pharmacy. Of course, we have our own post office, laundry, classrooms, and a library. There's a beauty salon and a barbershop." Dr. Bonner is ticking these off on his fingers. "Plus we have a tremendous food-service system and a fully operational farm, all staffed in part by our higher-functioning residents. Closely supervised, of course."

"It sounds like you're pretty self-sufficient around here," Dad says.

"Oh, indeed we are," Dr. Bonner says, rubbing his hands together. "Let's be off! We have much to see! All righty, folks?"

Mom is drooping. I can see it's hard even for Dad to respond with enthusiasm to match Dr. Bonner's.

On the way out I notice another family, a mother and a father and a girl about twelve, seated on a couch in the lobby. For a second I think maybe another doctor with a family is arriving. Then I realize that the girl doesn't seem quite right. She rocks from side to side, chewing on one fist. The parents look up anxiously as Dr. Bonner passes by.

"Someone will be with you folks shortly," he says to them, using a deep, reassuring voice. "A new admission," he explains quietly to us.

The girl catches sight of me and jumps to her feet, pointing and clapping her hands like a big, clumsy baby. "Girl!" she shouts. "Girl! My friend!" She looks back to her parents, who smile weakly and gesture for her to return to her seat.

I feel hot-faced and embarrassed, as if everyone is looking at me, waiting for me to respond, but I don't know what to do. Suddenly desperate for air, I look away and push ahead of everyone.

The wind has picked up and the sky is darkening. Mom pulls her sweater around her shoulders and shivers.

A large, bulky man, Dr. Bonner seems unaffected by the weather. "We're into a new recruiting phase here," he says. "While we appreciate the many foreign doctors who work with us, most of them are here only until they pass the board exams for private practice. The residents don't know the difference, but just between the two of us"—here he lowers his voice and leans toward Dad's ear—"most of the folks on staff here prefer to work with regular English-speaking Americans, if you know what I mean." Another wink.

"Sure," Dad says.

Dr. Bonner continues, "While it's still our policy for medical personnel to live right on the grounds of the institution, we realize it isn't always practical for whole families to live in an apartment here, as I do."

Dad is nodding genially.

"So," Dr. Bonner says, "we're building houses like yours here to attract a higher caliber of physicians who'll stay with us for a good long stretch, like you, Dr. May. I wish it could be something grander, but there are budget constraints when the state is footing the bill, you realize."

"Of course," Dad says. "It's perfectly adequate."

At this, Mom and I share a look.

"And you may not have discovered it yet, but we've even built a playhouse in back of your house for little Winnie." Dr. Bonner turns to look at me. "Although I can see you may be too old for it. Children seem to grow up faster these days."

"I'm thirteen," I inform him, emphasizing the *teen* part.

"The perfect age for a clubhouse!" Dr. Bonner booms.

"You'd like that, wouldn't you, Winnie?" Dad prompts me.

What can I say? "Sure. Are there any other kids around here, Dr. Bonner?" The memory of the girl in the lobby stabs at me. "Um, doctors' children, I mean."

"Ah, well, not yet, I'm afraid," Dr. Bonner says, squinting again. "You're the first. But we're hoping for more."

Dad squeezes my hand. "Soon, I'm sure."

By the time we reach the corner where Dr. Bonner points out that the school bus will stop for me, a steady drizzle has set in.

Mom halts abruptly. "I'm sorry, Dr. Bonner. I'm afraid I'm not up to this today. In all the confusion of moving, I couldn't find my raincoat and umbrella this morning, and I'm simply not prepared ..."

Dad wraps an arm around her. "You're already chilled, Colleen. Why don't you go on back to the house. Have some hot tea, if you can find those tea bags. I'll tell you all about it later."

"Quite all right," Dr. Bonner says a little sadly as Mom mumbles her regrets and hurries away.

"Winnie?" Dad says. "Are you still with us?"

"Yes, Dad. I was just wondering something." From this vantage point I can see down the main road that leads through an archway of gigantic elms, their branches leafless now, through the gated entrance to the grounds of the institution, and on into the so-called town of Bridgewater. "How far is it from here to my new school?"

"Not far," Dr. Bonner says. "From the main gate, over the bridge, maybe a mile and a half or so."

"Sure," Dad says. "Just down the street."

Just down the street. And worlds apart.

5

I tag along with Dad as Dr. Bonner parades us from building to building, pointing out various departments. The Bridgewater State School and Hospital isn't like any hospital or school I've seen before. Every building looks the same, from the red brick and barred windows outside to the hard gray terrazzo floors and pea-soup-green walls inside. The shadowy halls and stairways toss back echoes of every voice and footfall. Most of the rooms we see are lit by glaring fluorescent tubes. And I have to hold my breath; the smell reminds me of sweaty socks left in the bottom of the clothes hamper for too long, or maybe stale wiener water from day-old hot dogs.

But I forget all about the ugly colors and bad smells the minute we enter Watley Hall, home to the institution's youngest residents.

"These are the heartbreakers," Dr. Bonner says. "Not much we can do for them." He escorts us down the rows of cagelike cribs that house twisted little bodies with oddly sized and shaped heads, a few as small as softballs, many as big as lampshades. I hear myself gasp. I've never seen anything so grotesque! I try not to look, but these hairless heads with spots and sores are so close I could ... My hand moves toward one of the giant heads. What am

I doing? Suddenly I fear that the head might collapse or explode at the touch of my fingertips. The thought is sickening.

My own head feels dizzy, and I grab Dad's arm. The muscles feel tense beneath his suit coat. "Are you okay, Winnie?" he asks. I'm not even close to okay, but all I can do is cling more tightly to Dad. He pats my hand, keeping a firm grip on it.

From there we move on to visit wards with older kids wearing leather helmets to protect their heads during the uncontrollable, falling-down, drool-faced seizures they experience. We see adults who growl and bark, who wear diapers and have to be fed, who sit on the floor all day, rocking and banging their heads.

Dad and Dr. Bonner discuss lithium, lobotomies, and shock therapy.

It feels wrong to be staring at these people as if they were wild animals in a zoo, but they hardly seem human. I think it's the eyes. Zombie eyes! When I whisper this to Dad, he says they look that way because of the medicine they have to take, but I think it's more than that. Some of those eyes look back at me like they're begging to be set free.

I can tell that we aren't seeing the worst of it today. If the noises coming from behind locked doors and down off-limits corridors weren't enough of a clue, I would be able to tell by the exaggeratedly cheerful way Dr. Bonner steers us around, introducing us here and there, hustling us out before we see too much. The warning looks he exchanges with other staff members say more than his pleasant words. Even without a camera, he's like a photographer, giving us a carefully framed snapshot, not the whole picture.

Back from the tour, I kick off my shoes against the wall in the front entryway with a satisfying double thud.

"I'm in the kitchen," Mom calls.

I find her putting away dishes in the cupboards. Her apple-blossom canisters labeled *Flour*, *Sugar*, *Coffee*, and *Tea* are in position on the counter. Her collection of salt and pepper shakers parades along the windowsill. Perched on top of the refrigerator, the radio is tuned to pure static.

I feel steam building in my chest like a teakettle nearing the shrieking point.

"How was it?" Mom asks absently as she pulls a pair of cookie sheets from a box and hands them to me. "What all did you see?" Obviously her mood has been restored.

I slam the cookie sheets too hard back into the box. They crash like cymbals. "Don't bother unpacking any of my stuff, because I'm *not* living here!"

"Oh, Winnie, honey," Mom says, looking genuinely alarmed. "You should've stayed with me. I think maybe if we pretend we're sort of camping out for a while ..." She crosses the room toward me, but I stomp off to my bedroom.

"This place is a prison for freaks!" I yell, giving the door a window-rattling slam and throwing myself onto the bed.

I knew this place was going to be strange, but not like this. I expected it to be like a private school for kids who aren't quite bright enough for regular school. And the hospital part I thought would be just a regular hospital, to take care of the ones who get the mumps or need to have their tonsils taken out. I never knew places like this existed.

The stuff I saw today makes me wonder if Dad really knew

what he was getting into. How will he stand it day after day?

The stuff I saw today makes me wonder if even God knows what he's doing. Why are these poor creatures here on this earth at all? And why am I here with them?

The stuff I saw today—I wish I could rip it all out of my brain and throw it away! How can anybody look at it and ever be the same?

I press my face into my pillow and howl.

6

School has been in session here for a couple of months already. For me, it's the first day. I have a feeling I'll never catch up. It's not the schoolwork I'm worried about—that's always been easy enough for me. It's figuring out the pecking order and finding my place in it.

I take a deep breath and follow my new teacher, Mrs. Ames, into the classroom. Back home, I'd be in my last year of junior high. Here, there is no separate junior high school. Grades one through eight are all part of the elementary school. I'm about to become the twenty-sixth eighth grader in the whole school. In the whole *town*.

"Quiet down now, people," Mrs. Ames commands. She claps her hands briskly as she marches across the room, stopping front and center. I must look like a well-trained puppy, following closely at her heels and then halting obediently at her side. The twenty-five eighth graders fall silent, staring, some of them actually open-mouthed.

What are they thinking?

"We have a little excitement this morning, class," Mrs. Ames says. She sweeps the kids' faces with her eyes. Then she beams directly at me. "Meet our new student, Winona May."

Silence.

My face feels frozen. I clutch my notebook tightly to my chest and try to muster a smile. I've never been the new student before, never been the unknown in an established group. Am I supposed to speak first? "Hello." It comes out like a croak.

A wave of giggles and whispers rolls around the room. "Winona may what?" someone says.

At this, Mrs. Ames's piercing eyes snap up from the seating chart she's been consulting. "Manners, people! Now say a proper hello and make Winona feel welcome."

This time a few robotlike *Hello, Winonas* drift up the rows.

I glance around the room. My red-and-black-plaid shirtwaist dress and matching red patent-leather belt and shoes don't belong here. Enduring the scrutiny of the other girls, I suddenly regret wearing nylon stockings. My girlfriends back in Chicago started wearing them to school in fifth grade. Here, most of the girls are wearing white anklets and last year's corduroy jumpers and skirts with a telltale line where they've been let down at the hem. I long to find my desk. The teacher is taking forever.

"May I sit down now, Mrs. Ames?"

"Ah," Mrs. Ames says at last. Her finger is poised at the middle of the seating chart. "Here we go. Yes, you may, Winona May," she says in a singsong voice.

Giggles and groans break out around the room.

"Winona may, Winona may not," someone sings.

"Third row, third seat," says Mrs. Ames. "'May' goes between 'Marquardt' and 'Munson.' Let's make room, boys and girls. Move one of those empty desks into place."

More rumbling accompanies the pushing and shoving

required to get my desk into the right spot. Just as I'm finally about to slide into it, a boy pipes up, "What's that on her head?"

"It's her hat, of course," Mrs. Ames says absently, running through an attendance list. "Why don't you put it in your desk for now, Winona. I'll assign you a hook in the cloakroom later."

I'm not sure about cloakrooms; at my old school we had lockers. Part of me longs to melt into the crowd, another part feels an urge to establish myself in some small way. "Tam," I insist. Everybody knew that back home. At Morningside we all wore them. Don't these people know anything? I hold my ground and continue to stand beside my desk.

Mrs. Ames looks up from the attendance list and focuses her gaze on me. The classroom falls silent again and twenty-five pairs of eyes fasten on me.

"It's a tam," I repeat. "My hat is called a tam."

"Of course," Mrs. Ames says, a little too brightly. "Short for tam-o'-shanter, immortalized by the beloved Scottish poet Robert Burns." Mrs. Ames rolls her *r*'s, appearing to relish the sound. "Your family must be Scottish then, Winona, or Irish, perhaps?"

"She don't look Irish to me," comes a hoarse whisper that cuts off my response. "I seen her get off the Indian bus."

Shock ripples across the classroom. Just when Mrs. Ames appears ready to intervene, there's a knock at the door and she is summoned into the hall. "Monitor in charge," she says before leaving the room. "Janet Tyler."

In the row to my right, Janet Tyler smoothes her gray felt skirt, causing the shiny movable eye of the pink appliquéd poodle to shift and wink in the bright wedge of sunlight that stretches across her desk. Janet sits up straighter and cranes her head this way and that. She seems to be getting ready to take note of any infractions. Then, under her breath, she begins to mimic me. "It's a tam! It's a tam!"

Soon everyone is snorting with laughter. Someone snatches the tam from my head and begins tossing it around the room.

"Ew!" Janet sniffs when it lands on her desk. "I'll have to remind Mrs. Ames to hand out the lice combs."

My head swims in the laughter that swirls around me. I feel like the hole in a doughnut. Everybody around me is part of something, and I'm nothing, worse than nothing, the object of ridicule. *Whatever you do*, I tell myself, *don't cry.*

But I nearly do, with relief, when a thin, wiry girl in front of Janet swivels around, intercepts the flying tam, and tosses it back to me. I fall into my seat and stuff the tam into my desk, vowing silently never to wear it again. My rescuer rolls her eyes at Janet and fixes me with a gap-toothed grin. "I'm Paula," she says. "Where are you from, Winona?"

"My friends call me Winnie," I tell her, wondering if I'll ever have any friends again. "I'm from Chicago."

Paula's green eyes widen. "Chicago? Wow! Why would anyone want to leave Chicago for dinky little Bridgewater?"

"A big comedown. Indubitably!" Janet interrupts.

Paula ignores her. "Where do you live now, Winnie?"

Even this simple question makes me squirm. "Just outside of town."

"On a farm?" Paula asks eagerly. "We have a dairy farm. I showed my heifer at the state fair last year. Are you going to join 4-H?"

"Oh—well, I—"

"Wake up, Paula," says Michael Marquardt.

He shifts sideways in his seat, and I realize this boy is man-sized. Probably he's been an eighth grader before. His movement launches a pungent aroma, and I notice a thick rind of grime around his neck and ears.

"You never seen nobody in 4-H dressed like that," he says running his eyes over me. "She don't live on no farm."

"No, I don't."

"She lives on the Rez." This comes from Rodney Munson behind me. He punctuates his remark with a pencil jab to my spine.

"She must have been first in line at the missionary box," Janet says.

Why are they being so mean when they don't even know me? I'm being attacked and want to defend myself, but I fear that too much explaining will only make things worse. What could be taking Mrs. Ames so long?

"Well, where exactly is your place?" Paula persists. "If you ride the Indian bus, what else is out that way?"

"The colony," Janet says coolly. "She's probably an inmate at the colony."

At this, outright laughter erupts. A couple of boys fall out of their seats, writhing in mock convulsions. "Rootie-toot-toot," they chant. "We're from the Bridgewater Institute!"

"It's called the State School and Hospital!" I hiss. "And the people aren't inmates, they're residents!"

"So you're a resident?" Paula asks, drawing back.

"No! I just live there!"

"Well, if you live there," Michael Marquardt says slowly, as if he were talking to a baby, "don't that make you a resident?"

31

"Shh!" Janet orders, drawing herself up to monitor stature again.

Mrs. Ames strides into the room and drops a sheaf of papers onto her desk. "I hope the commotion I heard all the way down the hall meant that everyone was getting acquainted with our new student." She turns to the blackboard and picks up a piece of chalk. "Does the monitor have anything to report?"

Janet is already on her feet, her ponytail bobbing. "Yes, Mrs. Ames. Is it true she lives at the colony?"

I hold my breath, wishing I were invisible.

Mrs. Ames quietly replaces the chalk in the holder. She tugs at her skirt, as if to adjust some wayward undergarment. "Yes," she says, a wary look on her face. "Winona's father is a doctor out there."

My vision darkens at the edges. The way Mrs. Ames says *out there* confirms my worst fears. I've crossed some invisible boundary. A two-headed, green visitor from Mars would be more accepted here. Living on the grounds of the mental asylum places me not simply on the outskirts of town but in some unreachable zone, in some untouchable category. There will be no fitting in here for me.

I gasp softly when I feel the pencil jab at my spine again.

"That's handy," Rodney Munson whispers. "Your daddy can take real good care of you out there."

"Now," Mrs. Ames says, all business again, "who wants to read the morning announcements?" She scans the room for volunteers. "We're way behind schedule today, so I need a good reader who can clip right along."

My hand shoots up, almost of its own accord. I'll show them I'm not stupid or crazy.

"Winona," Mrs. Ames says, obviously startled. She hesitates a moment before handing the paper to me. "That's the way to start your first day. Jump right in."

Standing at the front of the room, I breeze through the announcements in a loud, clear voice without stumbling over a single word. I return to my seat, triumphant.

"Wow!" someone mutters. "She reads good."

To my right, I glimpse the slight shift of the pink poodle's shiny eye and hear a whisper, "For a retard."

7

I sit at the kitchen table, alone, stirring my Ovaltine and wondering how I can face another day at school. How could this happen to me? One day my life is fine, really almost terrific, on the verge of TV-show fabulous; the next day somebody changes the channel and I find myself in the middle of a tragedy, a horror movie. And there's no switching back to the old program. That one's been canceled, with no real explanation from my parents. Not even *Oh, sorry we wrecked your life.*

I've known some kids whose families were messed up. But not mine. I trusted my parents to keep our lives cruising along the same way they always did. Now *this!* Were they fooling me all along? How can parents pull the rug out from under you and expect you to act like it doesn't matter? Are we running away from something? Hiding?

I dunk a piece of cinnamon toast in my hot chocolate and take a bite. This *is* a perfect place to hide. We live nowhere. Our house has no address. We live outside the city limits, so we don't get a street name or number. We don't even get our mail at the regular post office. Just send my mail to Limbo.

It's the same with the telephone. The first time I looked at it, I didn't know what to do. Our phone has no dial! You pick it up and wait for an operator to say, *Switchboard.* You ask her for an *outside line.* Then you wait for another operator to come on the line and you tell her the number you want to call. Not that I have anybody to call around here; the Starlings, my faraway friends, are long-distance now.

When I said goodbye to them—which my parents gave me all of about ten minutes to do—they couldn't believe I was moving so far north, practically to the Canadian border. Would we even have electricity? Running water? Was I scared about living with the Indians?

When I asked Dad about all this, he said it was ridiculous, that Minnesota is as modern as any other state, probably more so than Alaska and Hawaii. But they got to be states only this year.

It turns out my friends were right about living with Indians— we live about five minutes from the Rez. Dad says it isn't a real reservation. It's just the side of town where a lot of Indian families live. I had never thought about there being Indians around anymore. I thought they were history. The Indian kids here aren't scary or mean, though; they just look beaten down and really poor. Nobody pays any attention to them at school, but at least they have each other; they're part of a tribe. I'm a tribe of one, and *my* life is history.

"Oh, you're up, Winnie." Mom startles me out of my thoughts when she pokes her head around the corner. "Well, have a good day at school." Then she goes back to bed.

Ever since we got here Mom's been in training for the sleep Olympics. She's run out of energy for unpacking and getting the house settled. She's hoping all this is temporary, too.

Dad has already left for work. What would happen if I didn't go to school? I've never skipped before, but the idea is beginning to appeal to me. The problem is that I have no place to hang out.

I decide it's time to check out my new so-called clubhouse.

Right away I see it's going to have a hard time passing itself off as anything other than a little kid's playhouse. It looks like a real Hansel-and-Gretel gingerbread house with shutters and window boxes and fancy curlicue trim all around.

I have to duck to get through the bright yellow door with *Welcome* painted across the top in red letters. Inside there's room enough for me to stand up straight, but just barely. Fake kitchen appliances are painted on one wall, a fireplace on another. Someone has even sewn and hung red gingham curtains at the windows. A small built-in booth occupies one corner, and along the back wall a ladder leads through a trap door to a tiny loft. Might as well take a look.

It's pretty cramped, hardly big enough for me to sit up without bumping my head on the slanted ceiling. But with a sleeping bag to soften the floor, it might be kind of cozy. From the small window near the peak of the loft I can see my bedroom window at the back of our house. It's not very far away, but because the playhouse sits at the bottom of a little slope, tucked behind some pine trees, it feels like a secret hideaway. Out here, I can imagine I'm anyplace in the world I want to be, which is anyplace but here.

I would have loved having a place like this when I was younger. Now, well, at least the Starlings can't see that the best thing in my life here is a cute little baby playhouse.

I go back to the real house to check the clock. If I'm going to school, I have to time my departure precisely. I don't want to have to stand at the bus stop too long. At this hour, aides lead dozens of residents in long, hand-holding lines from their wards to class-rooms in the main building. If I'm stuck there on the corner as they pass by, I'm a magnet for their gawking.

The sound of the back kitchen door swinging open behind me sends me leaping. As I whirl around, I bump the table and send waves of Ovaltine onto the floor.

A short, dark-haired man with wild, bushy eyebrows and weightlifter's arms strides into the kitchen with a large cardboard box. He wades through the spreading puddle of chocolate and sets the box on the table.

"Who are you?" I ask, backing away slowly. "Mom!" I call in the direction of the bedrooms. "Someone's here!"

The man stands in the middle of the kitchen, rocking from one foot to the other, cracking the knuckles of his hands, which are surprisingly small and soft-looking. His tongue bulges out of his mouth, as if it were too much for his lips to contain. His wide-set eyes dart nervously around the room.

"Um, what are you doing here? I mean, what's in this box?" I keep my eyes pinned on him and try to slow my breathing.

"Ch-Ch-Charlie. Charlie! My name!" he says, bobbing and ducking his head. "Gr-Groceries!" He lunges toward the box and I gasp.

"For Dr. M-M-May!" He opens the lid, revealing carefully wrapped and labeled packages of hamburger, chicken, and baloney. Eggs, butter, carrots, and potatoes. "M-Mrs. Wa-Walters told me. Okay?"

"Who is Mrs. Walters, Charlie? Why is she sending us food?"

"M-Mrs. Wa-W-Walters, kitchen b-boss! Ch-Charlie bring

food. Okay? My j-j-job! Ch-Charlie deliver food! Okay?"

"Yes, Charlie. Okay! Thank you!"

Abruptly, Charlie turns and leaves. But before I can catch my breath, he's back. "Milk!" he declares, setting two large metal cans with lids and handles on the kitchen counter. Then he's out the door.

This time I follow him. "Wait!" For the first time since we came here, I wish I had my camera. Maybe it's just as well that I don't; I don't want to scare him. "Wait, Charlie!"

At the sound of his name, Charlie turns. He may not look entirely normal, but he isn't repulsive.

"I'm Winnie. Dr. May's daughter. My name is Winnie."

Charlie ducks his head. "W-Winnie. Dr. M-May. Ch-Charlie back to work now. Okay?"

I watch as he goes back to his delivery cart and rumbles across the street. "Bye, Charlie!"

Back in the kitchen, I quickly put the food in the refrigerator and wipe up the spilled Ovaltine. Strange food. Strange people walking in. No wonder Mom would rather sleep through it all.

The time! Too much has slipped away. Not going to school is probably more trouble than just going. I grab my school bag and race for the bus.

The parade of residents crowds the sidewalk. In spite of constant scolding from the aides, they call out to me. They reach out and touch my hair, my clothes. I ask them to stop, but they pay no attention. I imagine this scene as a picture postcard sent back to the other Starlings. *Hello from Winnie and her new friends, the Loony-birds!*

If only I could fly away!

By the time the bus arrives from its stop at the Rez, I'm on the verge of tears. The door wheezes open. Aside from the driver's short bark of greeting, no one acknowledges me. I take my place in the empty front seat. The brief spell of Charlie's sweet baby-man charm has evaporated.

Another day in the twilight zone has begun.

8

Back home, everyone ate lunch in the school cafeteria; here, only the so-called farm dogs and Indians eat hot lunch. The townies bring cold lunch from home in a paper bag. And that bag had better not be too big or too little or some loudmouth will let you know it. The approved menu includes lunchmeat sandwiches on white bread, the squishy kind. Peanut butter and jelly is okay, as long as it doesn't happen every day. Maybe an apple or some carrot sticks, which must be ignored or ridiculed with a mothers-will-be-mothers shake of your head. And always a *store-bought* dessert. A squiggle-topped Hostess cupcake with creme filling is most highly prized. A coconut marshmallow snowball is fine for girls.

Today I think I have it right.

The lunch bell rings at 11:30, taking Mrs. Ames by surprise, as it does every day, though she must have been teaching for at least a hundred years. "My stars! It's that time already! Clear your desks, people."

I rise from my desk expecting to be carried along in the crowd of bustling townies heading for the cloakroom. Instead, I'm alone. Everyone stares at me. What have I done wrong this time?

When I catch up with the line moving down the noisy hallway,

I step in line next to Linda, a round, pudding-faced girl who is so polite that she's always apologizing and never quite talks out loud. "I'm sorry, Winnie," she whispers. "Why did you bring your lunch today? Did you forget it's Wednesday?"

Overhearing, Paula turns around. "Wednesday is always sloppy joes!"

In the cafeteria I take my place at a table with my perfect-any-day-but-Wednesday lunch and wait for the trouble to begin. It doesn't take long.

Janet Tyler places her lunch tray on the table and plunks herself down across from me. Her pink sweater set bears the monogram *JET* in the same fancy script she uses to plaster her initials all over her notebooks. "You just always have to be different, don't you, New Girl?" she says, looking around to make sure she has an eager audience. "But different isn't always better. Sometimes standing out looks stupid."

"Give her a break, Mrs. Jetson!"

I'm shocked to see that it's Gary, the class entertainer, Mr. Cool, standing up for me.

"She's from the colony," he reminds Janet in a whisper loud enough to be heard halfway across the lunchroom. "She's *supposed* to look stupid."

I feel my face heating up.

While everyone is cracking up, Paula stuffs a pickle spear into Gary's milk.

"Hey!" Gary says, taking a swig. "Dill-icious!" He swings the half-pint bottle in my direction. "Try this, New Girl!"

"Stop that!" says Paula. I'm grateful when she grabs the milk out of Gary's hand before he can *accidentally* pour it into my lap.

"And she does have a name, you know, if it isn't too hard for you to remember." Paula makes dagger eyes at Gary and Janet.

I shrug nonchalantly. "Never mind remembering my name. I won't be here for long anyway. My family will be moving again soon."

"Why, Winnie?" Paula asks. "Are you going back to Chicago?"

"Well, probably. But if not Chicago, somewhere."

Janet eyes me, obviously unconvinced, silently daring me to say more.

"My father's job here is temporary. Until the burns on his hands heal."

"That sounds awful!" Paula says. "What happened? Was there a fire?"

"No," I say, beginning to wish I hadn't started this whole explanation. "He has x-ray burns from holding patients under the x-ray machine. Before anyone knew it could hurt your skin."

"X-rays don't hurt!" Gary blurts out, sending a scattering of half-chewed corn kernels over the table.

"They can if you have too many," I explain. "That's why they took those machines out of shoestores. Remember when there used to be machines you stepped into and you could look at little x-ray pictures of how the bones in your feet lined up?"

Paula looks bewildered, but Gary brightens up. "Yeah! I saw one of those in the Dayton's department store in Minneapolis once. That was cool!"

"Well, they're not allowed anymore," I say. "At least not in Chicago. Because too many x-rays can burn your skin. That's what happened to my father."

"So what is he?" Gary asks, holding a carrot stick like a cigar and wiggling his eyebrows up and down. "A doctor or a shoe salesman?"

"A doctor!"

"Then how did he burn his feet?"

"Not his feet, his hands!"

"Why did he put his hands in the shoe machine?"

By now the whole table is listening and laughing. My cheeks are on fire. "He didn't burn his hands in a shoe machine! It was the regular x-ray machine that takes pictures of broken bones!"

"So how does that keep him from being a doctor?" Janet asks. "Doctors do more than take x-rays. And if he can't be a doctor in Chicago, why can he be a doctor here? And why would he want to work *out there* instead of at a regular hospital?"

My breath is coming fast. I have to get to the end of this before I lose control. "He's not just a regular doctor; he's a surgeon. Because of the x-ray burns, he can't scrub for surgery. At least until his hands have had time to heal. That's why we're here. His job *out there* doesn't require him to do surgery. *So,* as soon as his hands are better, we'll be moving on."

There! I've said it, just the way my parents told me to say it if anyone asked. *It's true enough,* they said. Still, saying it out loud makes me more uncomfortable than ever. People tell half-truths to hide secrets. I've never had to think of my parents as having anything to hide before. My stomach twists. I stuff my barely touched sandwich back in my lunch bag and get up from the table.

Janet is staring at me. "Moving on so soon, New Girl?"

Something about the way she looks at me with her x-ray eyes makes me feel like she can see straight through me.

9

I'm lying on my bed, shaking my Chicago-skyline snow globe. I glance up at the silver-framed pictures on my shelf of the five Starlings and try to imagine what the others are doing just now. Then Mom drifts into my room. She doesn't say anything, just drifts in and settles on the edge of my bed.

"I want to go back," I announce, keeping my focus on the glittering snowfall. Each flake is shaped like a tiny silver star.

"To visit, you mean? To see your old friends?"

"To stay!" I set the snow globe aside and lean up on one elbow. "And they're not my *old* friends. They're my forever friends! I want to live there, Mom, like we used to."

"I know."

"You hate it here, too. I can tell."

"We have to give it time, Winnie. We'll get used to it."

"I don't want to get used to—*this!* Why can't we go back?"

"We can't, that's all. There's nothing to go back to. The house is sold, and this is where your father works now. It's easier—for his hands …"

The questions of the kids at school are echoing in my head. "But why here, Mom? Why couldn't he get a different doctoring job in Chicago? I don't get it!"

"You don't have to *get it,* honey. We're okay here. Things could be worse."

"How? You and Dad don't know what it's like for me! Riding the Indian bus! And I don't have any friends! Everybody thinks I'm a retard! You just don't know, Mom! You never even go out!"

The more I rage on, the lower Mom's shoulders sag. I know I'm being a brat. Normally she wouldn't let me get away with it, but she's not herself here, not up to stopping me, and I don't want to stop myself. "If I have to stay here—" As I spit out the words, my mind races to think what the ultimate consequences will be, but just then my thoughts are interrupted by sounds at the door.

"Hello! I'm home!" Dad calls. "I thought I heard voices in here." He comes into the room and bends to kiss Mom and me, but I brush him aside. Mom nearly collapses into his arms. "Another long day," he says wearily. "How are my girls?" His tone of voice tells me that he's not sure he really wants to hear about it.

"Terrible! Everything is awful here, Dad!" I'm on my feet, pacing. "Moving here was a big mistake! Can't we go someplace else, even if it's not Chicago, there must be—"

"I have a commitment to fulfill here," Dad says.

"Do all doctors have to take a turn?"

"Well, no …"

"Then why do you? Why can't somebody else—"

"Five years," Dad says to me, still holding Mom close. "In five years you'll be eighteen and off to college. Anyplace you want to go. Until then …"

"Five years! I can't stand this place five more minutes! It isn't fair! I didn't ask to come here!"

"Children don't generally get to choose where they live," Dad points out.

"I'm not a *child* anymore!"

"You're certainly acting like one, Winnie."

"Ohhh! Well, when I'm a parent, I'll never—"

"Don't be so sure, Winnie," Dad says, gently stroking Mom's hair as they leave my room. "Don't be so sure." He closes the door quietly behind them. I open it and slam it hard.

I throw myself back onto my bed and press my fists against my eyes until I see stars. I pick up the snow globe again and shake up a blizzard that swirls over the Chicago skyscrapers.

I—don't—get it! Why would they want to live here? This place is like a bad dream! *You don't have to get it,* Mom says. And from Dad, *Children don't get to choose.*

But look what happens when they make the decisions! Why should I let them tell me what to do when they don't tell me why we're doing it? They're hiding something.

They're liars!

This thought sends me into a panic, the way I used to feel when a sudden power failure caught me in the dark alone. I want to scream for Mom and Dad to come and rescue me, but they could be communist spies, for all I know. Fugitives!

Maybe these so-called parents of mine have to stay here, but I don't. I still have my friends back home. Probably I could live with any one of the other Starlings for the school year. It would be like going to boarding school.

This new thought energizes me. Why didn't I think of it before? If I'd had any idea what things were like here, I would have insisted on it from the beginning.

I grab a notebook and start a letter to Pam, the leader of the Starlings. She's the one at the top point of the star. The star with a bright purple bird in the center—that's our official symbol. If I write to Pam and explain my idea, she'll pass the word around to the others, Cathy, Karen, and Roxanne. Maybe I can take turns staying at their houses. It'll be like a progressive slumber party.

November 20, 1959

Dear Pam,

Hi, it's me, Winnie, your long-lost sister Starling. I hated the way I had to fly away from the group on such short notice. I don't know what got into my parents to move us here. They must have been brainwashed or hypnotized or something. You can't imagine how weird this place is. I'll tell you about Ch-Ch-Charlie our deliveryman and all the creepy details soon. Believe me, you'll absolutely die! Also, I'm sorry I haven't written sooner. I just haven't had any good news until now. This is the good news—I'm coming back!

That's one of the reasons I'm writing to you, besides the fact that I really miss you guys! My parents are staying here a while longer. But I'm ready—really ready—to move back right away. So I'll need a place to stay. I'm hoping you can talk it over with the rest of the group and work out a schedule. A month here, a month there, however you want to set it up is fine with me. Won't it be great?

Thanks, Pam. I hope you'll write back soon! I can't wait to get back home where I belong!

Your "darling little star" (ha-ha),
Winnie

I reread the letter and feel a pang of guilt—why did I make fun of Charlie?—but I don't want to take the time to rewrite the whole thing. I fold the letter and stuff it into an envelope. I address it carefully and stick the four-cent stamp on upside down for good luck.

Then I look at the calendar and try to calculate how long it will take the letter to get to Chicago, how long it might take Pam to write back, and how long it will be before I'm gone from here. Maybe when I've left, Mom and Dad will snap out of the spell they're under and understand how wrong this all is. Maybe then we can get back to our real lives.

10

Back home I would never be up so early on a Saturday morning. Here, once that blasted whistle blasts, I can't get back to sleep. I wish I could escape into unconsciousness the way Mom does.

Dad, on the other hand, seems to have quit sleeping altogether. I find him in the dining room clutching a cup of coffee in both hands, staring out the window. I'm sure he hasn't heard me enter the room; I'm worried that I'll startle him. Instead, he startles me by speaking first.

"Good morning, early bird," he says, turning to face me. The bags under his eyes are beginning to make him look downright scary.

"Oh! G'morning." My voice feels thick, so I keep talking to clear my throat. "Isn't the sun ever going to shine again? It's been gray and gloomy nearly every day since we got here."

"People tell me this is fairly typical for November, except for the lack of snow. That should change soon." Dad rises from the table to fetch more coffee for himself.

I shrug. The weather here isn't important. I'll be gone soon anyway. I haven't mentioned my plan to Mom and Dad yet. But once Pam and the others have made arrangements for me, my parents will see how serious I am about leaving. I'm sure they'll go along with it. They have to.

Dad finishes pouring his coffee and returns to the table with orange juice and a danish for me. "Here's a day brightener for you, Winnie."

When I tap the danish on the plate, it makes a stale thunking sound, but I manage a smile. "Thanks, Dad."

He tweaks my nose playfully. "Not that. I have some news for you. An invitation."

My heart leaps. It's been less than a week since I sent my letter to Pam. Maybe her parents called mine and worked everything out to surprise me. I never imagined this would happen so fast.

"Oh, Dad! Thanks!" I jump up to give him a hug. "How soon can I go? I'm so glad you and Mom understand—oh, I want to start getting ready right now!"

"Whoa! Hold on a minute, Winnie. Don't you even want to know where you're going?"

I stop in mid-flight to my room. "Where I'm going? Oh, sure! Who called? The Winstads? Pam's parents?"

Dad looks confused. "Pam? No, Winnie. I'm talking about the Grandlunds, the people who manage the farm here on the grounds of the institution. They want you to stop in this morning and get acquainted, see the animals and everything."

"Oh."

"They invited all of us, but I'm on call at the infirmary until four-thirty, and it'll be nearly dark by then. So you might as well go and have a look."

I sag like a deflated balloon. "Can't I go another day? I'd rather wait until you can go with me." There isn't a question of Mom going anywhere anymore.

"A minute ago you sounded more than ready to get out of the house without us. Besides, the Grandlunds are eager to introduce a big-city girl like you to the country. They said they have a surprise for you. It wouldn't be polite to say no."

Another surprise. I'm not sure I can take many more.

"Winnie?"

"Mmm?"

Dad has moved to the telephone. "Will you go?"

"Oh. Okay." I have to pass the time some way until I hear from Pam. Maybe I'll take my camera along. So far, there hasn't been much around here I want to save on film, but there might be something worth looking at on a farm. Something not too weird.

11

By eight-thirty I'm heading toward the farm. Curtains of fog lift and fall, lift and fall, allowing only teasing glimpses of the unfamiliar terrain. The light is too poor for photos, but the familiar weight of my Starflash hanging from its strap around my neck gives my spirits a boost.

I pass the last of the residents' cottages. The sidewalk runs out, leaving me to follow a gravel path that winds toward the farm. I'm picking my way carefully around a stand of young pine trees when a man emerges from the midst of them.

"Hey, there, Dolly!" he calls, approaching me. He has a coil of rope over his shoulder, a bunch of burlap bags under an arm, a stout knife in one hand.

I run. Straight into a hedge. Before I can get to my feet, the man is standing over me. "You think I was the bogeyman?" His sharp blue eyes flash with amusement.

"No," I say, embarrassed. "You startled me is all, and um—" I try to pull my limbs from the tangle of branches, but thorns hold fast to my pants and jacket.

"Hold still now, Dolly. Stop struggling and let Vince help you." He drops his gear, pulls on a pair of leather gloves, and gently works each barb from my clothing. Then he lifts me to my feet. With his gloves removed again, he lingers over the task of brushing me off with his rough, grimy working-man's hands.

"Thanks, Vince." I back away, busily adjusting the camera strap around my neck.

"Nice camera, Dolly. You want to take my picture?"

I shake my head. "My name isn't Dolly. It's Winnie. I'm Dr. May's daughter. He's the new doctor here. I guess you work here, too?"

Vince smiles and shrugs. "Sure. I do what needs doing. Mostly gardening. Today I've been wrapping some of these little evergreens in burlap to protect them over the winter; snow could come anytime now. But it'll be somebody else's job to unwrap them in the spring." His smile fades, and he stoops to retrieve his knife. "I'll be gone by then."

I don't know what he means, but I don't want to stand here talking any longer. "Well, the Grandlunds are expecting me. The farm is this way, isn't it?"

"You're on the right path, Dolly. Just watch your step."

The farmer and his wife greet me as if I were their own granddaughter. They pull me into the kitchen with smiles and hugs and offers of gingersnaps and rice pudding. We sit at their round kitchen table, the two of them grinning at me over their coffee cups. Behind them I see window curtains, red plaid, identical to those in my playhouse, only larger.

After a few mild protests, the Grandlunds allow me to take their picture.

When I mention my encounter with Vince, they tell me he's a resident.

"How can that be? He told me he was leaving soon."

"Trial placement again?" Mr. Grandlund asks his wife.

She shakes her head. "Sometimes I think the ruling powers around here are a little short on common sense. Just because Vince can tie his shoes and plant a tulip bulb right side up doesn't mean he should be turned loose in the world."

"Is he dangerous?" I ask.

"Oh, no," Mr. Grandlund assures me. "I wouldn't say that. It's just that some of these people are never going to be suited to life on the outside. After being here too long, they don't even want to leave. This is home."

How long, I wonder, is too long?

"You just hurry on by when you see him," Mrs. Grandlund says. "That's the best policy with Vince."

After my barnyard tour, the Grandlunds tell me to wait on the back porch of the house while they fetch my surprise.

"You can come out now, Winnie!" Mrs. Grandlund calls.

I descend the back steps and see the two of them crouched down next to a wiggly, knee-high white creature with two stubs emerging from the top of its head. A goat.

"We thought you'd have fun with this rambunctious little fellow," Mrs. Grandlund says. "We call him Smokey."

"He's all yours!" Mr. Grandlund proclaims, as proudly as if he were handing me a shiny new bicycle. "What do you think?"

They must be joking. Why would I want a goat? How would I take care of it? Before I can find words, Smokey erupts with a series of high-pitched bleats. He breaks away from the Grandlunds and heads straight for me. I freeze.

"Smokey!" Mrs. Grandlund calls. "Grab him, Otto!"

"Hey, there, you little rascal—"

Smokey makes a beeline for my saddle shoes. With a few quick whipping motions of his head, he yanks out both shoelaces. He promptly devours them, then settles himself on top of my feet and gazes up at me with eyes full of innocence and trust. If it's possible for a goat to smile, that's what he's doing. My hands find their way into the soft fur curling around Smokey's ears. I feel myself smiling back at him.

"Now *that's* a picture," Mr. Grandlund says. "May I?" When the farmer reaches for my camera, Smokey leaps to his feet. Kicking and bleating, he dashes off into the surrounding woods.

Mrs. Grandlund sighs out loud. "You two go round him up. I'll get a bottle ready so you can feed him, Winnie. And remember to tell your mother that I intend to replace those laces."

Mr. Grandlund searches through the thickets. Because my shoes are floppy without laces, I stick to the path. It's dark in here, even in the middle of the day. "Smokey? Here, Smokey," I call.

Soon I step out of the woods into a clearing. I see stones set flush to the ground at evenly spaced intervals. Each bears a number. There are no names, but I know what this is. Though it doesn't look like a proper cemetery, people are buried here. Why in such a hidden spot?

I reach automatically for my camera. Just then, a slight movement near the edge of the clearing pulls my attention away from the stones. Someone slipping into the trees?

"Mr. Grandlund? Is that you?"

Silence.

Feeling the prickle of watching eyes, I turn to scan the area around me.

At first I think he's a statue. He remains so still, rooted to the ground, a peaceful little lamb placed here as a graveside guardian of all the nameless dead.

"Bleah!" the statue woofles sweetly. This is no gentle little lamb.

"Smokey!" I sink to my knees beside him. Someone has tied him to a bush with a leash fashioned from a vine. "Come on, boy. Let's get out of here." I free the line and lead him back through the woods.

When I meet up with Mr. Grandlund, I hand him my camera and he snaps a quick photo of me with my first pet. Most kids get a dog or a cat or a parakeet. I get a goat. My life here is ridiculous. I wish I had somebody I could trust to laugh with about it.

12

When I get back to our house, Mom is scuttling around the living room, stashing away everything valuable or breakable. "I don't know if this is a good idea, Max," she says to Dad.

"I thought you'd be pleased, Colleen. We've always had household help."

Mom heads down the hall toward the bedrooms; Dad trails behind. I follow them and turn off into my own room, where I settle on my bed to do some homework. Still, I can hear them.

"This place is so small, Max. I can take care of it myself. It's all I have to do."

"That's why I took Dr. Bonner up on his offer to arrange for some cleaning help. So you can get out and get involved in the community. Join some clubs or—"

"There's nothing here for me, Max. Besides, I'm just not comfortable with the idea of having a mental patient in our home, touching all our things!"

"Colleen, I've been assured that this woman is perfectly trustworthy, just a little slow." I hear a note of exasperation rising in Dad's voice.

"What if she has a fit or something? I don't think it's good for Winnie."

"Oh, for God's sake, Colleen, Vivian doesn't have seizures! She's perfectly harmless. Do you think I'd put you and Winnie at risk?"

"Well, it's thanks to you that we're here, isn't it?"

I can practically hear Dad biting his tongue.

Mom sweeps into my room, looking for precious items that need protection from the approach of the deranged cleaning lady. I pretend to be absorbed in my math problems, but I stay on the lookout from the corner of my eye.

With trembling hands Mom bundles my collection of porcelain figurines into a shoebox and stuffs them in the closet, along with my bank and jewelry box. Just as she reaches for my snow globe, the doorbell rings and the Chicago skyline tumbles through her fingers to the floor.

"Mom!"

It bounces off my book bag and lands with a heavy thud on the thick braided rug beside my bed. I dive to retrieve it. A furious storm rages through the Windy City, but the globe appears to be intact.

"Oh, thank goodness! Here, Winnie, let me—"

Mom reaches for the snow globe again, but I shield it. "I'll take care of it, Mom!" That's when I see the letter lying on my desk. The return address tells me it's from Pam. At last!

"Colleen! Winona! Come and say hello to Vivian. She's eager to get started."

Mom lifts her eyebrows at me, as if to say, *What can we do?*

"I'll be there in a minute," I call to Dad. As soon as Mom has turned to leave, I tear open the letter from Pam, expecting to see the usual doodles she decorates everything with in purple ink.

No doodles. No purple. Just plain pencil.

Dear Winnie,

I got your letter and thought you'd be interested to know that your old friend (ha-ha) Mary Ellen isn't at Morningside anymore. She isn't going to die like we all thought last year when she first got sick, but she fell down the stairs at school because of those ugly braces on her legs. I know she can't help it, but she really looks like such a spastic! She looks like she belongs at that weird place where you live. Now she has to have tutors at home. She might as well be back in that stupid iron tube thing. Can you imagine knowing you'll never go to a dance? I almost feel sorry for her. But she never fit in anyway, so maybe it's better this way. Like with your family moving on. It's interesting to see how people's lives turn out just the way they're supposed to, isn't it? Everything else is cool here.

Good luck at the Loony Bin!

Pam

P.S. Don't worry about the rumors that you left because you're PG. I set everybody straight about that.

What? There has to be more. I turn the paper over. Nothing.

"Winnie!" Dad sticks his head in the door. "Please come and meet Vivian now. You can read your mail later."

I put the snow globe back on the top shelf and follow Dad.

13

Staring out the window of the school bus, I can't think of anything but Pam's letter. She sounded so nasty. Is this some new phase, or have I forgotten what she's really like? I know the Starlings like to think they're much cooler than everyone else. But isn't it mostly a game, just a bunch of friends having fun?

The worst part about Pam's letter is what she didn't say. Not a word about me coming back. Nothing about me at all, really, unless she was telling me that I *deserve* to be stuck here. She couldn't have meant that. And the part about rumors of me being pregnant! She must have been joking, trying to sound funny and hip. She was funny, wasn't she? I used to think so when she was making jokes about somebody else.

I'm startled when someone slides in next to me. I turn to see the face of a boy from the back of the bus. Behind us I hear murmurs. Have his friends dared him to approach me? I stiffen in preparation for whatever challenge might come next.

He keeps his eyes averted and speaks so softly that I feel myself leaning toward him to hear.

"What do you call your goat?"

At first I think he's telling me some rude joke. I haven't told anyone I have a pet goat.

"What?" I demand of this boy in as harsh a whisper as I can muster. "What are you talking about?"

"I saw you in the burial place."

"Oh. Was it you who tied him there? Smokey is his name. How did you catch him?"

"He didn't take catching. Most things don't. Just watching and waiting."

"But what were you doing there in the first place?"

The boy shrugs and studies his hands. He doesn't seem to have nasty intentions.

"What's your name?" I ask.

"Justice. Justice Goodwater."

"I'm Winnie May."

"Winona," Justice Goodwater says, daring at last to look directly at me, if only for a second. "My cousin Charlotte is in your class. She told me about you."

"Oh. Yeah. Well, I just moved here. Temporarily. My friends call me Winnie. I like the—"

"I call you Winona."

We have arrived at school. The door of the bus whooshes open and Justice Goodwater is gone.

The first bell rings and I'm caught up in the rush for Mrs. Ames's classroom.

Justice is still on my mind when Janet Tyler corners me in the cloakroom and stuffs a slip of paper into my pocket. "Hey, New Girl," she says. "I'm having a slumber party Friday night and you're invited. Wear your best P.J.s and bring some of your favorite records to share." Leaning closer to my ear, she adds, "And your deepest secrets."

14

Friday night. Eight o'clock. I'm the last to arrive at Janet's house. I kept changing my mind about whether I wanted to go. I was going to make up an excuse, but Paula told me that Janet isn't such a bully-queen when she's not at school. Linda agreed and said Janet's parties are usually lots of fun. Between the lines, I got the message that it's not a good idea to turn down one of Janet's invitations. She'll make your life more miserable if you don't show up.

Carrying my overnight bag, Dad walks me to the front door.

"I'm perfectly safe walking up somebody's sidewalk by myself here, Dad," I tell him. "Probably there's never been a crime committed in this dinky little town. Everybody will think—"

"We've never met these people, Winnie. I just want to introduce myself."

I give up. He waits beside me until Mr. Tyler answers the bell.

"Bye, Dad," I say as soon as the door opens. "Pick me up early tomorrow." I grab my bag and scoot past Janet's father into the house.

The sound of voices and music leads me into a large room with gray-and-rose-colored carpeting on the floor and a wide brick fireplace on one wall. Paula and Linda are dancing. Heidi, another girl from our class at school, is there too. Curly-haired and with a mouth full of braces, Heidi is painting her toenails with one hand and eating popcorn with the other. Elvis is warning everyone not to step on his blue suede shoes. Janet is nowhere in sight.

I consider slipping out before anyone notices me. But as I head back down the hallway, I come face to face with Janet. "Hey, New Girl! I thought you'd chickened out!"

"Dad couldn't bring me till now," I fib. "Sorry to be late."

"Mother!" Janet yells into the kitchen as we pass by. "Winnie's here!"

Janet's mother steps out into the hall. "Well, hello, Winnie. I've heard so much about you."

"Oh, hello, Mrs. Tyler." I shift my bag from one hand to the other.

"Come on," Janet says, tugging at my sleeve. "Let's take your stuff up to my room."

She leads me upstairs to her bedroom, all flouncy with lace curtains and a ruffled canopy bed. I add my bag to the piles of the other girls' things, wishing I'd been brave enough to chicken out.

Back out in the hallway, Janet grabs my arm and pulls me into another bedroom, her parents' room. It's dark and smells of too-sweet perfume. It feels wrong to be here. "Janet, what are we—"

"Shh!" Janet whispers. "I want to show you something."

She steers me across the room to a bureau and slides open the top drawer. Keeping an eye on the door, she pulls out a box. She fishes out something in a flat wrapper and hands it to me.

At first I think it's a bandage of some sort, but as my eyes adjust I realize it's something else. Something private. As Janet sees this realization dawning on me, she says, "Just as I suspected, Miss Not-So-Innocent. I'd say it's time to move that fancy circle pin you always wear to the left side."

My hand goes to the gold circle on the right side of my sweater. I vow silently that I'll never wear it again. I try to give the thing in the wrapper back to Janet, but already she's stuffing the box back in its pointless hiding place.

"Look, Janet, just because I know what they are doesn't mean—" I hear muffled laughter from the hallway, where the other girls have gathered to witness this. A bitter mix of rage and embarrassment stifles my protest.

"Keep that as a little souvenir," Janet says, pushing me out of the room. "We don't want any little papooses now, do we?"

Papooses? Janet is outrageous! Has she been pumping Justice's cousin Charlotte for information about my conversations with him on the bus? I guess everybody really does know everybody else's business in a small town.

"Besides," Janet goes on, "my parents hardly ever use those things. Thank goodness! I mean, can you imagine anything more disgusting than your parents doing—*that!*"

"Ew! Not mine!" one of the girls declares.

"Well, I suppose they had to do it once to get you," says another.

"Gross!"

I allow myself to be swept along with the squealing group back downstairs, wishing I had the nerve to knock everyone down ahead of me like bowling pins. Along the way I drop my *little souvenir* into a potted plant, dreading the next get-the-new-girl trick.

•

Hours later, after too much ice cream, marshmallow crispies, and Coke, the five of us are sitting cross-legged, knee to knee, in a tight circle on the floor of Janet's darkened bedroom. Our attention is focused on Janet.

"The time has come," she says dramatically, producing a small bottle from behind her back. "Everyone do as I do," she instructs us.

We watch as Janet unscrews the cap and takes a sip from the bottle. The muscles in her face twitch when she swallows. Then she passes the bottle to Linda on her right.

Linda sniffs it.

"Drink," Janet orders.

"I'm sorry. I just don't know what—"

"Drink it *now* or leave the circle."

Linda drinks, shivers, and passes the bottle to Heidi.

Without hesitating, Heidi takes a swig. "Cooking sherry!" She tries to control a giggle that sets her curly hair bobbing. "Is that the best you could do, Janet?"

"What?" Paula cries. "No peppermint schnapps?"

"Shh!" Janet hisses. "You're spoiling the mood!" As Heidi passes the bottle to me, Janet continues to grumble. "Some days they lock the liquor cabinet. Some days they don't. How can I make plans when I never know what to expect? That's the way it is around here. They don't trust me; I don't trust them."

While Janet is distracted, I lift the bottle quickly to my closed lips and pass it on.

"Now," Janet says after she has recapped the sherry. "Is everyone ready?" She switches on a flashlight and shines it up into her own face. With her hair wrapped around big puffy pink rollers, Janet's head appears to float like a gigantic balloon. "It's time to reveal ourselves for who we really are, deep down inside where the light never shines. It's time to reveal our darkest secrets. Who will be the first to tell all?"

She places the flashlight on the floor and gives it a spin. The light flashes around the circle and comes to rest with its beam pointing at Heidi. Before she speaks, Heidi runs her tongue around the wires that embrace her teeth. The forbidden popcorn clings stubbornly.

"Well," she begins, "when I was maybe about five—no, probably only four—I was shopping with my dad at Hank's Hardware. And I really had to pee, and he kept telling me to hold it, but finally I couldn't wait any longer. So I found this toilet out on display, right in the middle of the store, and I didn't know any better, so—I used it!"

"You didn't!" Linda squeals. "Did anybody see you? Did it flush?"

"No, of course not! It wasn't hooked up. Everything leaked out onto the floor in a great big puddle! To this day, I refuse to set foot in Hank's."

Our shrieks of laughter are interrupted when Janet says, "I already heard that story from your brother. He says it happened when you were *eleven*."

At this, higher-pitched laughter breaks out.

"That's a lie!" the shamed one screeches, releasing a captive kernel of popcorn. "My brother wasn't even there!"

"No excuses," Janet insists. "Only the truth is spoken here tonight. Who's next?" She twirls the flashlight again.

As it rotates I begin to panic, suddenly aware that the game won't end until Janet has had a chance to belittle every one of us. I should have thought up something ahead of time. Now my mind is blank. Except for the one thing I don't want to share.

Most of the time I can keep it tucked quietly away. Like a forbidden word written on a piece of paper and folded over and over, pressed into a tiny square and zipped into a hidden pocket. Suddenly it's fighting to get out, to unfold itself, to reveal itself. The flashlight swings around the circle once more. This thing has become the biggest—no, the *only*—thing in the universe.

"Ahem," Janet says, gesturing toward the flashlight that is pointing directly at me. "We're waiting, New Girl. It's your turn to tell all."

"Well, I pass. Since this is my first time, I'll just observe."

"No deal," Janet says coolly. "That's why you're here. To learn by doing."

"Where I come from, sharing secrets is only for true-blue friends, not temporary ones."

"*Temporary?* So you think you're too good for us?" Janet asks. "Or maybe you're not good enough!"

"That's probably it," Heidi says, confident now that she has passed through the fire herself. "Maybe she'd rather hang out with those Indians on her bus. Or the other retards."

Paula and Linda exchange uncomfortable looks.

"It's not that," I say, my voice beginning to quaver. "I mean, *I'm* temporary. I'm not going to be here in Bridgewater for long. So—um—I won't have time to get to know you and become good friends like the rest of you. I'll be leaving soon, really. Going back to Chicago to finish the school year living with—ah—some of my old friends from my group—ah—back home in the city … at least until my family …"

It's crazy how the things I wish were true jump out of my mouth, while certain real-life things I don't want to face stay lodged inside me like a sharp fragment caught in my throat. I feel like a little kid who keeps claiming that her dog that got flattened by a truck will be home soon.

Looking around the circle of faces, at the hungry wolves waiting to devour my secret, I know there's no way I can satisfy them unless I reveal the last hidden thing at the bottom of my guilty heart.

But how can I possibly tell them the truth about what I did to become a Starling? How I pretended to care about the most un-cool girl at Morningside, Mary Ellen, when she got polio; how I went to visit her in the hospital and took pictures of her in her iron lung to show the curious Starlings; how I promised to come back to visit her again and didn't; and how I ignored her when she came limping back to school because by then I was a full-fledged Starling.

To do that, to tell that, is impossible.

"Nice try, New Girl," Janet says.

"What do you mean?" I ask, trying to calm the pounding of my heart.

"Everybody knows that the colony is the last stop. Nobody lives or works *out there* if they have any other choice. The doctors are as hopeless as the inmates. You're here tonight to tell us what really goes on."

"Yeah!" Paula chimes in. "Is it true that the doctors do secret experiments on the patients? Give them electric brain shocks and stuff?"

"Do they keep the dangerous ones chained up in underground dungeons?" Heidi asks. "I've heard sometimes they get loose and hide out down in the tunnels like alligators in the New York sewers!"

Experiments! Underground dungeons! What are they talking about? Dad wouldn't be part of anything like that, would he? I feel like I've done a belly flop and don't have enough air inside to speak.

"Quiet!" Janet orders the others. "Start with the tunnels. We know that what happens down there is bad. Give us the gory details. You must know something."

I've reached my limit. I'm going to get out of this town one way or another, so I don't have anything to lose here. I pick up the flashlight and shine it in Janet's face, creating a monster-sized shadow on the wall behind her big fat pink head.

"And how would you know anything about it, Miss Know-It-All? Have you ever been to the hospital? Do you know any of the doctors? Are you best pals with some of the residents? Tell us, Miss Big-Fat-Authority-on-Everything, how do you know so much about what goes on *out there*?"

Janet backs off with a look on her face that I recognize. It's the look of someone with a secret.

I switch off the light. The game is over.

15

Christmas comes and goes practically unnoticed at our house. New Year's Eve I spend eating a batch of Jiffy Pop and writing another letter to Pam. I can't understand why I haven't heard more from her. I have to keep trying.

Dear Pam,

Thanks for your letter! Too bad about Mary Ellen.

No! I don't want to say any more about that! I start over.

Dear Pam,

Happy 1960! Can you believe it? Not just a new year, a whole new decade! It's always exciting to imagine what a new year will bring. Like I said in my last letter, I'm hoping it will bring me back to Chicago. This is not just me day-dreaming. I really mean it. I'm serious about wanting to come back and finish the school year with the rest of you at Morningside.

Christmas here was so boring. And you won't believe what I got from my parents—a doll! Mom said she couldn't resist giving her little girl (me!) one more doll. It's called Barbie. Have you seen one? She's got long skinny legs and a tiny waist and big you-know-whats. In a way, she's pretty cool with all her cute outfits and high heels. Definitely a teenage doll, not a baby doll. But don't you agree we're a little too old for dolls? I hope your parents are letting you grow up on time. (Have you asked them yet about having me stay with you?) Sometimes I think my parents haven't figured out that at 14 (in one more month!) I'm not a child anymore.

Enough about my problems. I'm sure you were busy over the holidays. Probably that's why you wrote such a short note. Was there a snowflake dance in December? Who did you go with? What did you wear? I can't wait to hear all about it, but now we need to make definite plans for my return.

My New Year's resolution is to find a way to fly back to the Starlings so I can rejoin the flock. Please talk with the others and write again soon!

Your sister Starling,

Winnie

P.S. Don't tell anybody about the Barbie doll. I got a couple of Bobbie Brooks outfits, too. Perfect for sharing!

At school the novelty of my presence has worn off. Not that anybody is friendlier. I've become more ignored, more invisible.

"Poor Winona, the white pariah," Justice says when I mention this to him on the bus one morning. "Think of this as your chance to walk a mile in my moccasins."

I'm stunned by his words—too stunned to respond—even though I don't fully understand them.

"Do you know 'pariah'?" he asks.

"Um, it's some kind of snake, isn't it?"

Justice snorts. "Yeah, some kind of snake, all right."

For whatever reason, Justice is out of sorts today. I decide to let it go.

For a while I thought my invisibility at school was part of some silent treatment plot organized by Janet against the eternal New Girl. But ever since the slumber party, Janet hasn't been drawing attention to herself the way she used to. Every once in a while I catch her looking at me. I expect her to say something, but she looks away. I guess holding back on secrets—whatever she has to hide—can be enough to choke anybody. That's something I understand, but I hate thinking Janet and I are alike in any way.

I look at Justice's profile against the morning light coming in through the bus window. If the Starlings could see me with an Indian they'd say I'm getting desperate and must not realize how pathetic I look. But he's been a better friend to me here than anybody else has been so far. The thought makes me feel squirmy inside.

"You're staring at me!" Justice says suddenly. "What are you thinking?"

"Oh!" He's caught me off-guard. "Sorry. I was just—uh—wondering how old you are. I know you're a year ahead of me in school, but …"

"Fifteen. One more year. Then I'm gone."

"What do you mean? Gone where?"

"Gone from school. You can quit at sixteen."

"Why would you do that? You're too smart to quit! How will you get into college?"

Justice laughs.

"I'm not joking!" I insist.

"Yes, you are joking, Winona. Whether you know it or not. That's a joke."

His remark stings, but I feel too confused to protest. Justice turns away. He rests his head against the window and appears to doze.

At school we go our separate ways. It's nothing we've agreed to, or even discussed. It just seems to be something we both understand. Being friends with Justice doesn't exactly set me on the homecoming-queen path—some kids refer to us as Tonto and the Lone Retard—but with any luck I won't be here much longer.

16

After school the next day Justice is waiting for me when I get back from visiting Smokey at the farm. "Do you want to come in?" I ask as we approach my house.

He shakes his head. He never says yes to my invitations, but I keep asking.

"Okay. Wait here, then. I want to get my camera." I leave Justice scuffing his feet in the gravel of our driveway while I run inside.

I return with an extra sweater on under my jacket and my Starflash around my neck. "Where to?"

"The Spirit," Justice says, meaning the river.

The river borders the far side of the state hospital grounds. Officially, it's the Rye, named by white settlers for all the stills the bootleggers set up along the riverbank during the logging days. The Indians call it the Spirit River. Justice says it doesn't matter what word somebody puts on a sign. The stills are gone; the true spirit remains. A name that reflects the true nature of a thing is the true name.

There's no gate in the fence, but Justice knows places where the wire has been bent away from the posts. In a typical Minnesota winter, Justice tells me, it would be difficult to get through here.

Without snow, we squeeze under easily and make our way down the bank to the paths that run alongside the river.

I stop now and then to take pictures of birds and squirrels, of the bare birches and the red-coned sumac. We come to a sharp bend in the river where the water forms a swirling pool. Justice calls it the black eddy. I step out onto the ice that has formed along the edge. I want to get a shot of a fallen branch that bobs in the current at the open center. The ice seems solid enough. I take one step, then another.

"Stop, Winona!"

"What?" As I turn to face Justice, I hear noises under my feet, squeaks and pops.

"Don't move!" Justice orders. "Lie down. Slowly. And roll toward the riverbank."

"My camera ..."

"Lie down, Winona! Please—"

The catch in Justice's voice scares me more than the cracking noises under my feet. I lower myself to the ice. I wrap my arms around my camera to shield it and I roll toward the riverbank, where Justice crouches with outstretched arms. As soon as he can reach me, he grabs me by my jacket and drags me onto the frozen ground.

He leans close to me for a moment, breathing hard. "The water in the eddy—it cuts under the ice—it's like a thin shelf—you don't know how cold—how fast that water—"

"Okay, Justice. I'm okay. Thanks."

He releases his grip on me and drops down beside me on the ground to catch his breath. I turn my attention to my Starflash.

"Is your camera all right?" Justice asks after a moment.

"Um—yes, I think it's fine."

He nods, and we sit in silence again.

After a few minutes Justice asks, "Do you know that Winona is an Indian name?"

"Why would my parents give me an Indian name?"

Justice shrugs. "Winona means first-born daughter. It's what gave me the courage to talk to you. The girl on the bus with the Indian name who lives at the—hospital. I thought ..."

"What? You thought what?"

"I thought you might be able to find out about my mother— where they buried her. Which grave is hers. Which number."

"Your mother?"

Justice takes a deep breath. "When I was still a little kid, some white people came to our house and talked to my grandmother. They said they had my mother in custody, again—that she was a drunk and a danger to herself and to *society*. They had her committed to the state hospital for evaluation and treatment. Like they were trying to help her!"

"Was any of this true?"

"She drank some. Went on a binge sometimes, I guess. But she wasn't dangerous. She didn't drive a car, so she wasn't going to run anybody over. And she didn't get into fights. But we couldn't stop them. They'd already taken her away."

"Didn't you get to visit her? The hospital is practically across the street from you! How long was she there?"

Justice shakes his head. "I don't know. A couple of years. Finally, one cold January day like this, Grandmother got a letter saying she was dead. Dead and already buried. It had happened right around Christmas, but they waited weeks to tell us."

"That's awful! But—what happened?"

"There were rumors that she was afraid the doctors were going to fix her so she couldn't ever have any more babies—like some stray dog—and that she drowned in the river trying to get away, trying to get back home. We never heard anything official."

"Your grandmother didn't ask about it? A person has a right to know!"

"That's just it, Winona," Justice says, turning to look at me. "A *person* has a right to know, but not an Indian."

My mind tangles with outrage, sorrow, and guilt. Justice's mother, one of the nameless dead.

At the same time I begin to wonder if Justice has been making friends with me only to work up to this moment, gaining my trust so I'll help him get the information he wants. Once he gets that, will he walk away from me as quickly as I did from Mary Ellen? Or is my own guilt making me suspicious of everybody else?

For the first time I realize that our friendship probably costs Justice something, too.

17

Saturday afternoon I'm slumped at the dining room table. It's hard to concentrate on my science report about birds. Naturally, I chose starlings as my subject. I can't help being disappointed that everything about them isn't as pretty as I imagined. Starlings aren't at all flashy; they look a lot like crows, only smaller. Even their scientific name, *Sturnus vulgaris,* sounds, well, vulgar.

According to the encyclopedia, these birds aren't native to North America. Some guy who wanted to bring every type of bird mentioned in Shakespeare's plays to America imported them from Europe less than a hundred years ago. The newcomer starlings adapted and multiplied like crazy.

Starlings don't have the best reputation. They can be big bullies at the feeder, and sometimes they take over other birds' nesting places. But they do have some good qualities. For one thing, they're great singers. They can imitate other birds and even a cat's meow. Some people keep starlings in cages and teach them to whistle and talk.

While I'm learning this bird business, Vivian is busy bustling through the house with a dustcloth.

"What are you learning about today?" Vivian asks me when she passes through the dining room.

"Birds," I say simply.

"I got a parrot," Vivian says.

"A parrot?"

"Yup. It's not really mine, but I take care of him. Over at the canteen. I work at the counter there afternoons. Monday through Friday, one o'clock to four. I sell candy and gum and popcorn and soda. Five cents."

"What's the parrot's name?" I ask, happy to have a distraction. "Does it talk?"

"Oh, Popeye talks, all right. People try to get him to say all sorts of things. I'm teaching him the Lord's Prayer. He really listens to me. Arnie says I'm like his mama." Vivian blushes.

"Arnie?"

"He's my boyfriend!" Vivian giggles. "That's what *he* says. He asked me to go to the dance with him."

A dance? A boyfriend? A job? Vivian has a more normal life than I have! "What dance, Vivian? Where do you—"

"Ice cream!" It's Charlie, calling from the kitchen. "Ice cream!"

"Hey!" Vivian says as she goes to meet him. "We hear you, Charlie. You better not track in with dirty feet on this clean floor!"

"Hi, Charlie," I say, stepping into the kitchen behind Vivian. I reach into the box to see what he's brought.

"Ice cream! M-Melting!"

"Okay, Charlie. I'll put it away right now."

"F-Freezer! Ice cream goes in f-freezer!"

"She knows that!" Vivian flicks her dustcloth playfully at Charlie.

"Vivian," I say, "will you get the bags of dirty sheets and towels for Charlie to take? I think they're still in the bathroom."

"Oh!" Vivian cries. "I almost forgot!"

"You *d-did* f-f-forget!" Charlie says with a grin.

Remembering a chore of my own, I leave the two of them upstairs and head for the basement laundry room, where our dirty clothes collect at the bottom of the chute. Charlie always takes the linens and towels to the hospital laundry for us, but Mom doesn't want our clothes washed there. Lately she hasn't been interested in washing them either, so it's up to me.

I descend the wooden steps, blue alternating with green. The linoleum tile on the basement floor is a dizzy swirl of green and white. The air feels cool and clammy down here. Illuminated by a pair of eye-sizzling fluorescent tubes, the long, narrow room is filled with extra furniture and boxes of our stuff that doesn't fit upstairs. Dad calls this the recreation room, but recreation is supposed to be fun. I can't imagine there will ever be any of that down here.

Behind the stairway, a small, unfinished section of the basement has been set up as a laundry room with an automatic washer and dryer and a pair of deep washtubs. I pull a string that hangs from an overhead light bulb. The furnace takes up most of the space back here; its branching ductwork reaches out like octopus arms. A fuel tank and water heater stand along the far wall. Compared with the too-bright part of the basement, this corner feels cavelike, with its gray cement floor and cinder-block walls.

I dump out the contents of the basket at the bottom of the chute and sort the clothes into two piles, lights and darks. I place a load of whites in the washer and add a splash of bleach. As I'm re-capping the bottle, the top slips out of my hand and rolls out of sight. Darn!

Fortunately it doesn't take me long to find the cap, near the fuel tank. When I bend to pick it up, I see something I haven't noticed before. In a narrow recess in the wall is a heavy metal door. I try the knob, but it's locked. Why is there a locked door down here? Why hasn't Dad said anything?

But I think I know how to get into the mystery room. Dad is terrible with keys, so he often hides one near where he needs to use it. I stand on tiptoe and feel around the doorframe. Sure enough, my fingers close on a key. I slide it into the lock, turn it, and lean into the door.

Immediately I'm swallowed by darkness. As I wait for my eyes to adjust a little, I hold on to the door with one hand to make sure it doesn't swing shut behind me. I reach out to the right, then the left. The cinder-block walls on either side feel close. It must be some kind of a storage room, but I don't see anything in here. It would make a great darkroom for developing pictures.

I've always wanted to try that. Most people send their film away so they can get color pictures, but I like the details you get with black-and-white. You'd think all the shades of gray in those images would make a picture fuzzy, but it works just the opposite way. It makes everything look deeper and clearer. You end up with more, not less.

Suddenly I'm aware of a faint draft pulling at me from the deep end of this inky space. This is no closet; it's a passageway. Maybe Dad doesn't know about this door after all. I shiver to think that the things Janet and the other girls were saying at the slumber party about dungeons and underground experiments could be true. If I ask Dad about it, can I trust him to tell me the truth? Do I want to know?

My heart begins to pound and my head swims. If I let go I might tumble into this tunnel like Alice in Wonderland falling down the rabbit hole.

18

At four thirty in the afternoon Mom is still in her bathrobe. I can't remember when she last washed her hair. When I offer to do it for her, she looks at me like I've offered to set it on fire.

I try to cheer her up with a funny story about Mrs. Ames. I imitate the way she tugs at her girdle while she writes on the blackboard, but Mom's sad, blank face doesn't change.

Then Dad walks in. Mom is sitting on the couch playing solitaire on a TV tray. I'm stretched out on the floor watching Annette and Bobby and the rest of the Mouseketeers singing and dancing their hearts out.

To get our attention, Dad drops the mail on the coffee table with a noisy slap. "How are my girls?"

I wait for Mom to answer first, but of course she has nothing to say. It's up to me to fill the silence. "Fine."

Dad lets out a sigh.

I get up and head for my room, claiming to have tons of homework to do, but Dad stops me.

"If you have time to watch TV, I think you have time to help your mother with dinner."

As if she has any intention of actually cooking. It's been frozen TV dinners around here for weeks. "She needs help with more than dinner," I mutter as I make a U-turn toward the kitchen.

"Skip the sarcasm, please, Winnie. It doesn't help."

"But it's not fair, Dad! I have homework to do. She does nothing!"

"Your mother is having a tough time adjusting here," Dad says in a low voice. "We all are, Winnie. But I have my work to distract me, and you have school."

"Oh, right! School is a great help! Everyone hates me!"

"Not *everyone*."

"What's that supposed to mean?"

"I understand there's someone you spend quite a lot of time with. Obviously *he* doesn't hate you."

"Smokey?" I say this just to be contrary. I know exactly which someone Dad is referring to, and I've been dreading this conversation.

Dad casts a cautious eye toward Mom, but she seems totally absorbed in finding a red Jack to put on a black Queen. Dad motions for me to follow him into the kitchen. He slides into a chair at the table while I lean against the stove with my arms crossed. "Sit, Winnie," he says, pointing at a chair across from him. "Please."

Good dog, I praise myself silently as I take my place, bracing for the lecture.

Dad takes a deep breath. "Winnie, I learned in medical school that people are all the same under the skin. Same blood, same bones, same organs."

I shudder at the thought of the peeled-back look of the bleached-out dead bodies medical students have to dissect.

"In fact, our skin is an organ, too, the largest organ of the body.

As long as we live in this world, we can't just slip it off like a jacket. We have to wear our skin. We can't keep it hidden inside with our lungs and our heart, or do without it like our appendix."

I tap my foot impatiently.

"Our skin is the part of us that other people see first, and based on what they see, they make assumptions, judgments."

"Well, that's not fair!"

"Winnie, when people look at—your friend …"

"Justice."

"When people look at Justice, they see an Indian, a representative of a group that not many generations ago resented and resisted our presence here. Many of our American ancestors fought and died trying to establish a civilized—"

"Dad! I can't believe you're saying this! You don't know Justice! How do you even—do you have somebody spying on us?"

"No spies, Winnie. And I'm not saying I necessarily agree with this point of view. I'm only telling you what I know is in the minds of many people when they see you with a young man from the reservation."

"Dad! You're the one who said it isn't a real reservation! Besides, it's not like I'm going to marry him! We're just friends! We talk!"

"Can't you talk and be friends with other kids? Someone who's more—like you? Like the friends you had back in Chicago."

"It wasn't *my* idea to leave them, Dad. I don't have any choice here. The kids in town think I'm contaminated. They don't want to be friends with me. They think I'm a freak!"

"That can't be true, Winnie. You went to that slumber party not long ago. I'm sure there'll be other invitations if you just try harder to make friends with the right kind of—"

"This is ridiculous, Dad!" Suddenly I'm on my feet.

Dad holds up his hands as if to ward off my verbal blows. "I don't want to argue about this, Winnie. And I'm not saying you can't talk to the boy. I just don't want your life to be more difficult than it has to be. I don't want you to get hurt. That's all. Think of how your mother—"

I've heard enough. I walk out the back door, feeling a need to run with long strides and breathe big lungfuls of cool air.

19

Since our blowup, Dad hasn't said anything more about Justice. Maybe he feels guilty about interfering in our friendship, but more likely he's trying a different approach. I think he plans to keep me occupied, too busy to hang out with an Indian.

"I think you'll find this interesting," Dad says to me as I tag along beside him through the halls of the administration building. "It could be an opportunity that changes your whole outlook on things here."

"Could be," I say, thinking, *Don't hold your breath.*

Dad raps on a half-open door with a sign that says *Social Activities Director* on it, and we step inside. A woman at a desk is talking on the telephone and picking up cake crumbs from a plate. Her eyebrows fly up when we enter, but she continues her phone conversation. With one chocolaty finger she indicates for us to be seated.

The nameplate on her desk says *Marsha Flomm*. Short, straight dark hair frames her round face. The thick lenses of her glasses give her a slightly goggle-eyed look, but her cheerful patter on the phone, punctuated with brief bursts of laughter, makes me relax.

She concludes her phone conversation and wipes her fingers

on a napkin. "Well, goody," she says, pushing herself away from her desk. "Dr. May and daughter have arrived!"

When she stands she doesn't seem any taller than when she was sitting down. Dad and I rise and take turns shaking her chubby hand.

"Miss Flomm," Dad says, "thanks for taking time to see us. This is the daughter I was telling you about. Winnie."

"Winnie! What a darling name!"

I decide to take a chance. "Thanks, Miss Flomm, but I'd rather be called Winona."

Dad's eyebrows twitch a little at this declaration, and Miss Flomm hesitates for an instant. The two of us give a sigh of relief when Dad doesn't say anything.

"I understand, Winona," she says. "Eventually those childhood nicknames are best reserved for family use. And please call me Marsha or you'll make me feel like an old lady!"

We sit again, but Marsha bounces up immediately. "Help yourselves to gumdrops," she says with a giggle, holding out a candy dish.

Between gumdrops and giggles, Marsha fills us in on social life at the institution: twice-a-week movie nights, a dance every two weeks, bowling, volleyball, softball, picnics, holiday parties, hayrides, carnivals, live theater, assembly programs with acrobats, animal acts, and clowns, outings to the Dairy Queen. The social activities director is nearly bursting with glee by the time she finishes describing all the fun she organizes.

"It sounds as if you provide the residents with plenty of distraction, Miss Flomm," Dad says.

"I've never seen any of these things going on," I say.

Marsha looks suddenly serious. "It's been my experience that people generally see only what they want to see, or what they expect to see. A lot of folks think the *fluffy stuff* isn't very important, but the residents are much happier when they can participate in the same kinds of leisure activities that we all enjoy. It's normal to want to have fun!"

"I'm sure that's true, Miss Flomm," Dad says. "Now maybe you could describe some of the volunteer opportunities you mentioned to me earlier. With your full schedule, I can understand why you need a little extra help."

Ah, now I see what Dad is up to. Keep Winnie busy.

"I need all the help I can get!" Marsha says cheerfully. "We're always looking for volunteers to take the snack cart around. We load it up at the canteen with candy, popcorn, sodas, magazines— it's a good-will thing, letting the employees in the far-flung departments and cottages know we haven't forgotten about them. That would be a good place for you to start, Winona. You'll learn your way around and get acquainted with everybody. It's perfect!"

Dad is nodding and smiling. "Sure. After school. And Saturdays. She really has plenty of free time. Sounds interesting, doesn't it, Winnie? Um, Winona?"

While I'm struggling for an answer, Marsha says, "There is one thing I should probably ask, Dr. May. You don't mind your daughter traveling through the tunnels, do you?"

The tunnels! I shoot a look at Dad. He doesn't flinch. He doesn't say, *What tunnels?* He *knows* about them, and he's sending me down there!

I feel like all the air has been sucked out of the universe, but no one else seems to notice.

Marsha jabbers on. "It's too difficult to maneuver that clumsy old cart from building to building over the curbs, especially in bad weather. It's much easier to go underground. We provide training, of course, before you go out on your own. And a whistle! In case you get lost or—anything."

"Dad, I don't know …"

"It's perfectly safe, Winnie. I use the tunnels all the time."

"Everyone does," says Marsha.

"Sure," Dad says. "Those tunnels are the lifeblood of the institution, like our own veins and arteries. Remember what they told us last year on our Disneyland tour, Winnie? All the dirty work that keeps the park running takes place underground. People never see it; most of them don't even know about it."

I wait until later in the evening, when Dad and I are doing the dinner dishes, to tell him about my discovery of the mystery door in our basement. The look on his face tells me he's surprised that I know about it. So it's not like he just forgot to mention that our house has a direct connection to the secret underground world here. Even after our tunnel discussion with Marsha, he didn't bring it up.

"Why didn't you tell me about it before, Dad?"

"I didn't think you needed to know, Winnie. It doesn't concern you."

"Does Mom know?"

"Yes, of course she does."

"Why? How does it concern her?"

Dad lets out a sigh of exasperation. "She's an adult, Winnie. She's entitled to know. Besides, having that connection to the tunnels is one very attractive feature of this place. It's like having our own bomb shelter, in case the Soviets come calling. Or a tornado."

"Da-ad!"

"Well, I hope we never have to use it for that," Dad says. "But tell me, Winnie, how long have you known about the door downstairs?"

I shrug. "Not long." Before Dad can ask any more questions, I have one for him. "Is that door the way you come and go through the tunnels, Dad? I don't see you going into the basement very often."

"Oh, no, Winnie. That door is strictly for emergency use. In case I'm called at home in the night or during bad weather."

"But you said it's safe for me to take the snack cart through the tunnels. You said—"

"For official business the tunnels are safe. Miss Flomm will show you the ins and outs of your route. But I don't want you exploring the tunnels on your own. It's no funhouse, Winnie. That door in our basement is to remain locked at all times. Understood?"

"Understood."

I drop the subject, but I know I haven't gotten the whole story about what goes on down there. I have only the snapshot version.

20

After a few training sessions I'm on my own. I stock the cart at the canteen and roll it down to the end of the hallway. Ready or not, I turn the key and lean into the heavy door.

The tunnels are dimly lit. Some sections are shadowed in nearly total darkness where caged light bulbs have burned out and not yet been replaced. Fat, hissing pipes run along the ceiling. Some stretches are stifling hot; others are cold and damp. The wheels of the cart make a low rumble.

It feels like a dream world down here. There are no signs, only number codes painted on the walls at major intersections of this underground maze. The passageways must be meant for people who know their way. I have a confusing map and, as Marsha Flomm promised Dad, a whistle—in case I get lost or *something* happens and I need to call for help. Even so, I feel ill equipped and unprepared.

The sharp echo of a door closing in the distance makes me jump. I'm dizzy with panic. I'm not ready to do this!

When a pair of aides escorting residents in wheelchairs appear from a side tunnel up ahead, I want to throw my arms around them and beg to be rescued. They smile and nod as we pass each other, as if we're all strolling through a park. I take a few deep breaths and keep moving.

At last I find myself emerging into the bright lights of the hospital kitchen. Everything is shiny stainless steel and gleaming white tile. Daylight streams in through broad windows. Workers wear white uniforms, white shoes, and full-length wraparound white aprons. Some have tall white baker's hats. I am giddy with relief. This isn't where I was headed, but I feel as if I've arrived in heaven.

"Charlie!" I dash over to him, happy to see a familiar face. He's stacking empty crates beside a trash bin.

"W-W-Winnie!"

Charlie takes me to his kitchen boss, Mrs. Walters, a stout, gray-haired woman with the powdery complexion of someone who spends her days in a flour bin. Her eyes widen when they land on me. "Well, Charlie, who do we have here?"

"W-W-Winnie!"

"I'm Dr. May's daughter."

"Oh! Dr. May! He's already a favorite around here," Mrs. Walters says. "And he talks about you all the time in our staff dining room."

He does? That's a surprise.

"This place must be a little strange for a young girl to get used to. And for your mother—especially living right here on the grounds. I have an apartment here too, you see. When I first started, I never thought I'd stay, but twenty-two years later, here I am!"

"Twenty-two years?" The thought is mind-boggling.

"My husband worked over at the laundry till he retired a few years ago."

"M-Mr. Wa-Walters! Laundry!" Charlie blurts out.

"Oh, the laundry!" I say. "That's where I'm supposed to take the snack cart today."

To my relief, Mrs. Walters sends Charlie with me. "Charlie probably knows the system better than anybody. He'll help you get your bearings."

I head back into the tunnels with Charlie proudly in the lead. The hitch in his walk reminds me of Mary Ellen and her first day back at Morningside wearing a baby-blue mohair sweater and those awful braces on her legs. The worst part was the look on her face when I flew past her in the hall, in a hurry to catch up with the other Starlings, without even saying hello.

21

The first time I roll the snack cart into Cottage 14, I want to abandon the cart and run out screaming and never go back.

Cottage 14 is the place where they keep the adult women residents who are the most difficult to control. They wear shapeless sacks for clothes, and they all have the same bowl-on-the-head haircut. Most of them make angry animal sounds and look so fierce that I expect their eyes to pop out of their heads.

"Don't be scared," the charge nurse says to me. "These ladies aren't going to hurt you. They're just curious about outsiders. Same as all of us."

I nod and try to smile as she accompanies me down the hall.

"When we heard Dr. May's daughter was coming to be our snack girl today, the aides couldn't believe it. You're something new, missy!"

I wait for the nurse to unlock the wide metal gate where several residents have gathered to stare at me. "Back off now, shoo!" she hollers at them, banging a clipboard against the bars. "Go on, I said! Move!"

Grumbling, the women retreat to the far side of the large, bare room. "Okay, missy," the nurse says to me. "You can bring that cart into the day room now."

Three aides reading magazines occupy the only furniture. I wheel the cart into the room and jump when the door clangs shut behind me. A surge of hot and cold runs through me like electricity.

The nurse laughs.

"Aren't you coming in with me?" The thought flashes through my mind that this woman might leave me here locked in, purely for entertainment.

"Somebody has to stay out front. But don't worry. I'm not far away. Give me a shout when you're ready to leave."

"Okay. I won't be long!"

"Oh, you take your time, missy. Get acquainted." She ambles away, keys jangling at her side.

I glance at the aides, who look so sullen and bored I'm not sure I feel any safer with them here. "Hi," I squeak.

Having gotten to their feet, the aides circle the cart, talking quietly among themselves. "Why any doctor's kid would come in here if she didn't have to is beyond me," one mumbles.

I don't care if they don't want to talk to me, I just want to get this over with and get out. *Hurry up!* I urge them silently as they inspect the offerings.

At the same time I try to keep an eye on the residents, who seem to be pushing closer. One tiny woman who has been scuttling around the room like a crab, totally naked, latches onto my ankle. "Oh! Can someone help me here? Please!" I manage to say.

One of the aides waves a hand at me. "Oh, don't worry about Rose. She likes to sniff everything out. Nosey-Rosey, blind as a bat since she was born and she's been here ever since."

"Blindness is the only reason they put her here," says another aide. "But after so long, she's as loony as the rest."

"How old is she?" I ask as Rose clings to my leg with her wizened face turned up toward mine. She could be fifty or maybe even one hundred.

"Twenty-nine," an aide tells me.

I hold my breath as Rose feels her way up my body till her hands reach my face. Her fingers flutter lightly across my cheeks, nose, and forehead. Then she drops back down to her crouched position on the floor. When she turns to scoot away, Rose bumps into the snack cart. Startled, she bounces up against the legs of one of the aides, then another. They reach for her.

"Careful there, girl!"

"Slow down, Rose!"

Rose freezes. She whimpers and begins to wiggle her fingers in front of her face, as if she's looking for a glimmer of light or movement in the shadows. Suddenly she jabs at her left eyeball until it pops out of the socket and dangles by a shiny white cord-like thing on her cheek.

I turn away, nearly strangled with nausea.

"No! No!" one of the aides shouts. "Bad girl, Rose!"

I hear a slap, followed by sounds of a struggle. A whistle blows. Other residents in the day room start shouting and jostling one another to see what's happening.

"Charge!" someone calls. "We need restraints here!"

The charge nurse comes running.

As soon as the door is open I push past her. Someone shoves the snack cart out after me. "I'm sorry," I mumble. "I didn't mean to—"

"You run along now," the charge nurse says. "Rose gets a little agitated sometimes. She'll be fine."

I look back and see Rose being wrestled into restraints. She looks so scared, so small and helpless, entirely at the mercy of the overpowering aides. I have an urge to scream at them to be more gentle. There must be a better way.

I leave Cottage 14 with the snack cart and a fresh load of guilt. As much as I hate the thought of returning, I vow to try once more. For Rose's sake. For Mary Ellen's. For mine.

22

After a few more visits to Cottage 14, I'm getting toughened up. As soon as I'm inside the day room, I give a little two-note whistle to get Rose's attention. Then she crab-walks over to me and settles herself up against me while I talk. It doesn't matter what I say; she just likes to hear my voice.

"Lunchtime!" the charge nurse announces as she approaches with her ring of keys. The smell of food drifting in from the dining room reaches the day room, and the residents rush for the door. "Come on, gals. Line up nice, now."

The only time Rose is willing to wear clothes and walk upright is at mealtime. If she refuses, she isn't allowed to eat. Food is the main thing these residents have to look forward to.

When I start to follow along, the charge nurse stops me. "No need for you to get in on this, missy," she says. "You can wait in the hall; we'll be done in no time."

From around the corner I watch as Rose gets herded into the dining room. She manages to find her way to her place at the table. Then, like all the rest of them, she's tied into a chair, arms behind her, until an aide comes by and shovels the food into her mouth. This is done as quickly as possible, just to get it over with.

I think the only reason the aides put up with me is because of Dad. They've never had to deal with a doctor's kid hanging around their little universe before. They're polite enough, but I get the feeling they think I'm snooping around and spying on them. Then again, they don't mind letting me take one resident off their hands for a while.

With Dad's help I have permission to take Rose outdoors after lunch today. I didn't mention that Justice will be part of the expedition.

Rose hasn't left Cottage 14 for as long as anyone can remember, except to go to other parts of the institution—the dentist's office or the infirmary. I've brought a wagon for her to ride in, since she's not too keen on walking upright even in familiar surroundings, much less in the big wide world.

At first the charge nurse seems skeptical. "Well, well, missy. I have my doubts about this, but I can't quarrel with doctor's orders, so here's your girl."

I'm relieved to see that Rose has been dressed in some sort of jumpsuit she can't get out of. I give her a few minutes to identify me again with her nose and fingers.

"Bring her back when you've had enough," the nurse says.

I lead Rose outside and get her into the wagon. She rides along with her face turned up and her mouth held in the shape of an *O*, as if she's in a state of constant wonder. We head to the nearby playground, where Justice is waiting.

"Here we are! Justice, this is Rose."

"Hello, Rose." Justice squats beside the wagon to let Rose touch his face and get his scent. The sad, faraway look in his eyes makes me wonder if he's thinking about his mother. I don't ask.

"Let's have some fun," Justice says at last.

We try to get Rose out of the wagon, but she won't budge. We end up pulling her around the grounds, up and down the sidewalks, singing every silly song and nursery rhyme we can think of. Rose holds on tight to the sides of the wagon, rocking happily back and forth.

When the wagon goes over a curb, Rose laughs out loud. After that we go out of our way to hit a few more curbs. "Bump-bump!" Justice and I sing, just to hear that short bark of delight again.

Then we search for a hill, a gentle one. Justice shakes his head. "I'm not sure this is a good idea, Winona."

"She's having a great time!"

"We can't let her go flying down a hill all alone."

"I know that! I'll go with her."

Justice clucks over us like a mother hen as I climb into the wagon in front of Rose. Instinctively she wraps her arms tightly around my middle. I grip the handle for steering on the way down. "Just keep it straight," Justice orders.

"Ready!" I yell. Justice gives the wagon a gentle shove.

The ride is short and easy. At the bottom Rose rocks fiercely, indicating that she wants to go again. Again!

After a few rides we're ready for something more. Something bigger. "You know every rock and tree around here, Justice. Take us to the biggest hill you can find!"

"This is pretty flat territory," Justice says with obvious reluctance.

I keep prodding.

"Well, there is the Mill Hill. Along the river, at a place where a flour mill used to be. Kids go sledding there in the winter. The problem is, it'll be a bumpy ride without snow. I've never seen anybody go down it in a wagon."

"Maybe nobody ever thought of it before," I say. "Let's go take a look."

The Mill Hill is steeper than I was expecting. There aren't any trees to worry about running into, but there is the river at the bottom.

Justice turns up his collar and shoves his hands in his pockets. The wind is chilly at the crest of the hill. "I don't want to have to jump in the water to save the two of you."

I'm too caught up in this adventure to let caution slow me down now. "I'll drag my feet. We'll stop long before we get to the river. Come on!"

Justice positions the wagon. I settle in the front, with Rose hugging me from behind. My heart pumps as wildly as it used to when I rode the big roller coaster at the amusement park back home. I miss having fun, just plain old fun.

"Take it easy now, Winona," Justice says. "Don't wait too long to start dragging your feet."

I grip the handle and we're off. Flying!

"Hang on tight, my little Rosey-Posey!" I call over my shoulder. Out of the corner of my eye I catch a glimpse of Rose's fringe of hair being lifted by the wind, and of her wide-open mouth trying to swallow this thrilling new world whole. In that instant, the right front wheel hits a rut. We jackknife. The handle flies out of my grip and sticks in the ground in front of us, launching Rose and me head over heels down the slope.

We roll to a stop, limbs tangled, laughing, laughing.

I look up into Justice's panicked eyes when he reaches us.

"Winona! Is anybody hurt? I knew I shouldn't let you go! Are you—?"

"We're fine, Justice! Everything is fine!"

For the first time since we moved here, I'm happy. It had been so long that I'd almost forgotten what that feels like. I try to imagine telling the other Starlings about this. Not making a joke or a creepy story out of it, but telling them how good I feel when I'm with Justice and Rose, how good *life* feels when I let go of myself.

But as soon as I start thinking of the Starlings, my pure happiness fades.

23

As usual, the six o'clock whistle blows me out of bed. I hope it's the one and only time I start my birthday like this. February 3, 1960. It's been a whole year since Buddy Holly died in a plane crash, along with Ritchie Valens and the Big Bopper. Three famous singers, heading to Minnesota, all gone at once. I hate having an anniversary like that on my birthday. It's hard to know how to feel when the good and the bad get mixed up together.

The good part is I'm finally fourteen. I like the sound of it, even though I thought I'd feel different, more grown-up by now. I always expected there would be some magic age when I'd feel I had *arrived,* like crossing over a bridge, and suddenly everything would make sense and that lost-like-a-little-kid feeling would be gone. Now I know that if there is a magic age, it isn't fourteen.

In the still half-dark kitchen I find a birthday card from Mom and Dad next to a muffin with a candle on top. I pour myself some orange juice and strike a match. *Happy birthday to me,* I sing softly. I don't have to think hard to come up with a wish. *Wings!* To fly away from here. But where? How? I know I miss being part of a flock, but fledglings don't fly back to the same old nest. It's been so long since I've really been a Starling, maybe I don't fit there anymore. I'm not cheering myself up at all. I blow out the candle, eager to get this stupid birthday out of the way.

"Happy birthday, honey!"

I'm shocked to see Mom up so early. She crosses the kitchen and plants a quick kiss on my forehead. Dad is right behind her and adds his kiss on top of Mom's.

"You started the party without us!" Mom says, picking up my burned-out candle. "I hope your wish comes true."

"Not necessarily," Dad teases me. "You still have to go to school today."

The school day passes. I haven't told anyone it's my birthday, not even Justice, so I don't have to feel let down when nobody says anything.

After school, I change clothes and head to the farm to see Smokey. I'm hoping to find Justice waiting for me along the way, but he's nowhere in sight.

Back at home, I find Mom all smiles and buzzing around the house. She's dressed in a nice skirt and blouse and has even done her hair and put on lipstick. It's great to see her like this, but after getting used to seeing her so stuck in the doldrums, I'm not sure I can trust this sudden change.

"Well," Mom announces when I settle down in front of the television. "I'll just go downstairs and check on—um—the laundry."

"Do you want me to do it?" I ask absently as Dick Clark introduces the American Bandstand kids to the next new danceable number by Bobby Darin, "Mack the Knife."

"Oh, no! You relax, honey. You're the birthday girl."

I hear Mom's high heels tap-tapping down the basement stairs. Soon I hear her voice. "Winnie! Oh, Winnie, would you come down here for a minute, please?"

She probably needs me to show her how to run the washer.

My foot has barely touched the green and white linoleum floor when a flash of light blinds me. A small chorus of voices reaches me through the spots swimming in front of my eyes. "Surprise! Happy birthday!"

I sit down hard on the bottom step, waiting for my vision to clear. Clustered around Mom are Paula, Linda, Gary, Rodney, and Susie, a girl from class I've hardly talked to before. The furniture and boxes have been pushed into some sort of order. Loops of crepe paper hang from the ceiling.

"Oh, Winnie," Susie says, hiccupping with laughter. "You should see the look on your face!"

"Yeah, you can close your mouth anytime now."

"Shut up, Gary!" Paula hisses.

"Just so she doesn't drool on the cake," Rodney adds.

Mom ignores all this. "Are you surprised, honey?" She comes over to pull me to my feet. "I invited all your classmates, but you know how it is at the last minute, you can't expect everyone …"

I tune out the rest of her babble, thinking only that this can't be happening. I have to get out of here. I want to die.

Linda comes over to me, looking concerned. "I'm sorry, Winnie," she whispers. "But are you okay? I mean, you aren't going to throw up or anything, are you? You look pretty pale."

Afraid to use my voice, I just shake my head.

"Who's that?" Gary says, staring over my shoulder. "Your father?"

I turn and see Charlie descending the stairs. He's carrying two large boxes.

"Ch-Charlie bring food," he says to no one in particular.

"Okay! P-P-Party f-f-food to Dr. M-May!"

Mom tells Charlie where to put the food—way too many sandwiches, ridiculous amounts of fruit salad and baked beans, and an enormous cake. Mrs. Walters must have thought the whole school was coming to my party.

"Help yourselves now, kids," Mom says.

My guests have backed themselves into a horrified huddle in one corner.

"Don't be shy," Mom says, waving her hands in frantic circles.

No one moves.

"You too, Charlie," Mom says, trying to shoo him in the direction of the table without touching him. "Help yourself to something before you go." This isn't like Mom, this desperate need to make something happen.

Charlie shakes his head vigorously. "No! No f-food for Ch-Charlie. P-Party foo-food for Dr. M-May, M-Mrs. May, W-W-W-Winnie!"

At the sound of my name exploding from Charlie's mouth in this way, Gary comes to life. "W-W-W-Winnie!" he hoots. "W-W-W-Winnie!" Soon the others pick up the chant. "W-W-W-Winnie!"

Charlie rocks from side to side. His head bobs. Mom's smile is slipping. She doesn't know how to handle this.

Gently I take Charlie by the hand and lead him up the stairs. "Thank you, Charlie," I say. "You did a good job."

"G-Good job! Okay! Ch-Charlie bring food!"

From the back door I watch Charlie trundle off. I consider going back inside. I know I should, for Mom's sake. Instead, I dash across the backyard, intent on hiding myself.

By the time I reach the playhouse, I realize how cold I am without a jacket. I think of the sleeping bag in the loft. I open the door and squint into the darkness, wishing I'd brought a flash-light. I feel my way up the ladder and push open the trap door.

"Happy birthday," says a voice.

"Justice! You scared me out of my wits!"

He laughs. "What are you doing out here? Is your party over so soon?"

"What are *you* doing out here?" I pull myself up into the loft beside him and wrap one side of the sleeping bag around my shoulders.

"The sky is clear tonight," Justice says, pointing out the tiny window. "I thought this would be a good place to keep a lookout for shooting stars or flying saucers."

"Like me, you mean, flying out of my own house. How did you know about this?"

"I ran into Charlie earlier this afternoon. He spilled the beans."

"Yeah," I say, feeling a tide of tears welling up. "Well, he did more than that ..." I'm glad for the darkness so Justice can't see me looking like a crybaby.

"Here," Justice says, pulling a small bundle of newspaper out of his jacket. "I brought you something."

Inside I find warm fry bread, fragrant with cinnamon and sugar. "I'll share it with you," I say.

As we nibble the fry bread, I tell Justice for the first time about my life in Chicago and that I want to go back. He listens, but the look on his face tells me he thinks I'm whining. The more I talk and try to explain, the more I sound like a whiner even to myself, and the less convinced I am about what I really want.

When I stop, Justice says, "Your life here isn't so bad, Winona. It's just more—real."

"Why do you say that? My old life was real!"

"It sounds more like a fantasy world to me. It didn't teach you much about the rest of the world. About people with bigger problems than what to wear to the country club."

"Well then, I'm not sure I like *real*." This conversation is making me feel stupid and shallow.

Justice shakes his head slowly. "You're fourteen. Time to grow up."

"Maybe so, but I don't have to do it here," I say, still feeling stubborn.

"Growing up in a hard place makes you stronger—makes you grow up faster."

"Good. The sooner I can get out of here, the better." I try to say this with conviction, even though I feel my defensiveness fading.

"Well, for now, I'm glad you're here, Winona."

I feel a tingle inside when Justice says this. In spite of the cold, my face and neck feel hot. In the darkness I'm brave enough to respond, "I'm glad *you're* here, Justice."

24

For several days after my party, I lie low, with a so-called sore throat. Dad doesn't take my temperature or even bother to ask me to open wide and say *ah*. I knew he wouldn't, so it's easy to get by with this. Fooling ourselves this way is an unspoken agreement between us.

I've never even *been* to the doctor. I'm probably not up to date on my shots or anything people get checkups for. I'm lucky *I* wasn't the one to get polio, instead of Mary Ellen. Dr. Dad doesn't like to acknowledge that anyone in his family could be sick. I'm sure he's never called in sick, ever. Sickness is weak and messy; it's for other people. He's the one who fixes it.

Mom doesn't argue. She writes my excuse without even looking at me. She's the one who's beginning to look sick. I've never seen her so thin and pale.

I know Mom meant well, but the whole surprise-party idea was doomed from the beginning, just one more reminder to everybody of what a misfit I am. I can't bring myself to apologize to Mom for running out.

My first day back at school, Janet corners me in the girls' bathroom. "I heard a lot about your party," she says.

Something in her voice is different. She doesn't sound as superior and snotty as usual. She's not talking in her usual loud voice, the one that most people use only when they're addressing a large audience. Her eyes keep darting toward the door, keeping track of who comes and goes, who might be overhearing us.

"Well, you didn't miss anything." I try to elbow my way past her, but she steps in front of me.

"Well, yeah, everybody said it was totally weird, and for once I'm glad my parents didn't let me go. But there's something I've been wondering about." She looks around, waiting for a couple of younger girls to leave.

I wait with her, figuring I might as well get this over with.

"The patient who delivered the food," she whispers, leaning toward me, even though we're alone. "Um, how old is he?"

"Delivered the food? At my party? I don't know how old he is. What's the difference?" I try again to leave, but she grabs my arm.

"Well, how old would you guess? I mean, what does he look like?"

"Charlie? Why do you—?"

"Oh, his name is Charlie? Well, never mind." Janet straightens up. "Nobody said. They just told me some retarded guy who couldn't talk right came in with the food."

She's gone and I'm left standing here without a clue.

When I get home from school, I hear voices coming from Mom and Dad's bedroom. The door is shut. I lift my hand to knock, but then I realize Mom is crying. Dad's voice is low and soothing. I drop my hand and listen.

"It's all right, Colleen, everything will—please don't cry—I think it's for the best, too—you should go as soon as possible—I'll make the arrangements—don't worry about Winnie, she'll be fine here with me—I'll tell her something—no, no, she doesn't have to know that part—please, Colleen ..."

I tiptoe into my room and close the door. Mom is leaving! Is she sick? Dying? Getting a divorce from Dad? Becoming an ambassador to Timbuktu? Anything is possible, and who knows what they'll tell me. I can't figure out if they think I'm grown-up enough to be fine no matter what they do, or if they think I'm still just an easy-to-fool little kid. Either way, I'm not going to be told what's really going on.

I never imagined my family could fall apart this way. I don't know how I'm supposed to act. What if somebody asks about my mother? How can I say she's gone? Not having a group of friends is embarrassing; not having a mother around is scary.

I pull out one of my photo albums and flip through the familiar pages, longing to climb back into them. If I could take a picture of myself sitting here now, the caption would be *Winnie waiting for the next lie.*

When Dad comes into my room I brace myself for an elaborate fib. It turns out to a simple one instead. "Your mother is going to visit her sister Cassie in Philadelphia for a while," he says.

"Okay."

"I think a little vacation, a change of scenery, will be good for her. She's been pretty low lately."

"Uh-huh."

"She feels bad about—um—going away without us, especially you, Winnie. She knows you aren't very enthusiastic about this place yet either."

I shrug and keep flipping the pages of my photo album.

"Mom probably won't say much to you, Winnie. I told her I'd explain things and you'd understand. You and I will be just fine here on our own for a while."

"Sure, Dad." Behind the lids, my eyes are beginning to burn. I keep them turned down, looking at the photos without really seeing them.

"Well, good," Dad says, patting me on the back and trying to sound cheerful. "It's settled. Everything's fine."

As soon as the door closes, I'm up and pacing, willing the tears away. If Mom can leave without any explanation, so can I. She and Dad think telling me any old half-truth is good enough, so I guess it doesn't matter what I tell them either. Or don't tell them.

I can't wait any longer for Pam. I'll write a letter to the other Starlings and send a copy to each of them—Cathy, Karen, and Roxanne.

Dear sister Starling,

Hi! It's me, Winnie! I hope you haven't forgotten about me! I think of you all the time and wish I could get back there as soon as possible. I really want to finish the year at Morningside, so we need to decide which of you I can stay with first.

I already wrote to Pam about this, so you can talk to her about it and let me know whose place I can start at. It'll be just like our round-robin tennis matches. I can't wait for our never-ending sleepover to begin!

Please write back as soon as you can.

Your lonely sister Starling,

I hesitate over how to sign my name. Winnie? That's how the Starlings know me, but it sounds babyish to me now. And who is this new Winona? Maybe I'm finally growing into my real name, but right now I feel like a double exposure, like a ghost hovering in two worlds and not belonging to either.

25

In the three weeks since Mom left, Dad and I have been walking around like robots. We go through the motions of school and work and eating dinner and watching TV. But it doesn't feel like living.

I've been avoiding Justice and Rose and even Smokey. Dad and I haven't had much to say to each other either, but he's been having a lot of late-night long-distance telephone calls. I've become a good eavesdropper.

If I dared to pick up the receiver in the hall while Dad's on the extension in the bedroom, I might get the whole story. Or I might get caught. So I take notes on what I can pick up through the wall and try to figure out the missing parts on my own.

Tonight I should be studying for a social studies test. Instead, I'm sitting on the edge of the tub in the bathroom next to my parents' bedroom, waiting for the sound of Dad's telephone voice to begin on the other side of the wall.

Meanwhile, I review my list of the things I know so far:

1. Mom is in Philadelphia, but she's not staying with her sister. She's at Brandywine Manor, a private hospital for people who have nervous breakdowns and the money to pay for treatment.

2. Dad was suspended from private medical practice because of some *incident* in Chicago.

3. Dad is making plans. Plans to leave Bridgewater, which he calls a *failed experiment*.

Here's what I need to know:

1. Is Mom ever coming back? If she is, when?

2. What happened in Chicago? Is my father a criminal?

3. What happens next, and where do I fit into it?

I keep looking over my notes, trying to solve the puzzle of our lives, but too many pieces are missing and I can't imagine how it will ever turn into a whole picture, much less a pretty one.

The ringing phone alerts me to take up my listening post. I press one ear tightly to the wall and clamp the palm of my hand over the other ear.

"Colleen, sweetheart," Dad says. "How are things going today?"

Mom! Now I can't resist. I slip quietly out of the bathroom and down the hall to the other phone, where I ease the receiver out of its cradle. I hold it lightly to my ear and try not to make any breathing sounds.

"Things are fine here, too," Dad says. "Still no snow. I guess this will be a rare winterless winter in Minnesota."

"It's spring here," Mom says. Her voice sounds as soft and light as a sleepy child's. "The wisteria is blooming."

"Are you getting outdoors?" Dad asks. "Getting any fresh air?"

"When Cassie comes to visit, we go for walks. It's very pretty here. Peaceful."

"Good, Colleen. That's great to hear. And your doctor tells me you'll be ready to return to us soon."

"Oh, Max, I don't know …"

"I miss you, honey. We both do."

"How is Winnie?"

"Fine. She misses you, but she's doing fine."

Hearing my parents talk this way makes me feel uneasy. Their conversation sounds so strange, so—polite. They're being so careful with their words, as if using the wrong ones might break some fragile thing they're both trying to hold on to.

"Would you like to speak to Winnie?" Dad asks. "I know she'd like to hear your voice. Hold on a minute, Colleen. I'll put her on the line."

I hang up as quietly as possible and dash back to the bathroom. By the time Dad knocks on the door I'm making splashing noises at the sink.

"Winnie! Finish up in there! Mom's on the phone and she wants to talk to you."

"Okay, Dad! I'm coming."

When I get back to the phone I feel out of breath, nervous about talking to my own mother. I wish it had been her idea to talk to me, instead of Dad's suggestion.

"Hi, Mom," I say, trying to sound normal.

"Winnie, honey. Hello. How are you?"

"Fine, Mom. I'm okay."

"Good. How's school?"

"Oh, you know, it's school. It's fine."

"Good. I'm glad to hear that."

Finally I can't stand it. "Mom, um—when are you coming home?"

Dad is giving me a pointed look, but I continue.

"I mean, I know you needed a little rest, but—um, it's been

weeks and—ah—there's a parents' thing at school soon and I wondered, do you know when …"

"Oh, Winnie," Mom says in that faint little voice. "I don't know. I don't think I'm ready. Of course I want to see you, but—going back to Bridgewater, well—I'd better talk to Dad about that."

I want to reach through the phone and shake her. Shake her till she wakes up out of this trance she's in and acts like my mother again. "Okay, Mom, sure. Well, I'll put him on. Bye."

I hand the phone to Dad and head for the door. I don't want to be here anymore. I just want to take off and disappear.

I start walking toward the farm, through the woods, and past the state cemetery. I haven't gone this far in this direction before, and I feel like I'm crossing a boundary into new territory. Just beyond a low, swampy area of tamarack trees, I arrive at the Rez. Scanning the assortment of broken-down cars and trailers everywhere, I have a hard time telling where the junkyard ends and the living space begins.

In someone's dirt front yard, I come across an old pickup that's lost its doors and wheels. The way the truck sits so low to the ground makes it look like it's sinking into the earth. I recognize a couple of younger kids from the bus playing in the back.

"Hi," I say. "Can you tell me where Justice Goodwater lives?"

They point across the road to a small house not much bigger than our garage back in Chicago. It looks as if it hasn't seen new paint for a century. The front porch is held up with cement blocks, and as I approach, an assortment of skinny hounds come bounding out from under it and greet me with tail-thumping enthusiasm.

In a matter of seconds the front door opens and Justice steps outside. "Winona!" The dogs turn their attention to Justice, but with a snap of his fingers he sends them back under the porch. "Welcome to the Rez. As you can see, no teepees, no savage redskins dancing around the fire with tomahawks, plotting the next raid on the white folks."

Justice is grinning, but I'm not in the mood for his teasing. I shake my head and look away, wondering if it was a mistake to come here. He takes a step toward me. "Winona? What is it?"

"My mother," I whisper. "She's gone, and I don't think she's coming back." Saying this makes my knees feel like they can't hold me up any longer. I lower myself to the top step of the porch. Justice sits beside me. I'm not dressed warmly enough and I begin to shiver.

"You're cold," Justice says. "Want to come inside?"

"No, thanks. I can't stay. I just stopped to tell you I'm—leaving."

Justice moves closer. I smell the rich, smoky scent he carries on his clothes and hair. "What do you mean, leaving?"

"Um—running away." I wish I could think of different words. *Running away* sounds like something a six-year-old would say. "I can't stay here anymore. I'm so—miserable!"

Justice nods. "I've tried it a couple of times. Running."

I turn to look at him, to see if he's joking. "You have?"

Justice nods. His eyes look serious.

"Did you come back on your own?"

"Less than a week later. Both times."

"Why? What happened?"

"Nothing," Justice says. "That was the problem. The worst of

119

the stuff I thought I was leaving behind came trailing along with me. Inside. It's like dragging a heavy suitcase. When you're on the run, there's no place to put it down."

We sit without talking for a minute. Off in the distance, we hear strains of Pat Boone from a transistor radio. *Lipstick on your collar's gonna tell on you-oo.*

"Your father is good to you, isn't he?" Justice asks.

"I guess so. I'm not sure he tells me the truth about every-thing—"

"But he treats you okay?"

I nod.

"I'll walk you home, Winona."

"Okay."

Behind us, I hear the whimper of the dogs until we're out of sight in the tamaracks.

26

By the time I get back to the house, I'm starved. Dad is in the kitchen making sandwiches and whistling.

"Winnie! I was about to send a search party for you. It's pretty brisk out there. Did you have a good walk?"

A good walk? I was ready to run away and he asks if I've had a good walk?

"How about something to eat?"

His good mood is so annoying I want to scream, but I'm too hungry to say no. I stand at the counter and gobble a sandwich of liver sausage and sweet pickles on rye. Dad takes his to the table. "Don't you want to join me?" he asks.

My mouth is full, so I shake my head and continue to eat standing up.

"Suit yourself," he says cheerfully.

After a few minutes of chewing he says, "I think we're finally turning a corner here, Winnie. I know things looked pretty bleak for a while, especially when Mom first went away, but now I get the feeling that changes are on the way. Big changes."

I swallow hard. "What kind of changes?"

Dad turns up his palms and stretches out his arms. "All kinds. This is an election year, you know. A new president in the White

House will bring new ideas. There's a lot of unrest in our country right now. Everybody's challenging the status quo."

I'm so exasperated that I nearly choke. "Dad, what does this have to do with us?"

"There'll be big changes in the medical field, too," Dad continues, pushing his chair back from the table. "I've been talking with several of the docs I knew in med school—the research that's going on is amazing! Whole new kinds of drugs are on the horizon to treat people with epilepsy, schizophrenia, and depression. Probably within the decade the big state hospitals like Bridgewater will shut down entirely."

This catches my attention. "What will happen to the residents? Where will they go?"

"Out into the community. Some of them will still need special care in smaller residences, but many will be able to attend regular schools and hold jobs. No more dumping all the mental misfits in these big warehouses. It'll be a whole new world!" Dad takes another sandwich and munches happily. "Get us some orange juice, will you, honey?"

I sigh out loud, thinking maybe Dad is crazier than his patients. As I open the refrigerator door, I try to imagine Charlie and Vivian living on the outside. Even if the great new medications make their behavior more normal, they still won't exactly *be* normal.

I cross the room and get two glasses out of the cupboard. The farm, the canteen, the beauty shop, movies and dances with people who know them and like them just the way they are—the residents' whole little world will be gone. Who will they be without that? Plenty of things about institution life need to be fixed. But all the safe, familiar parts of the life the residents share—that's a lot to ask them to give up. I should know.

I pour the juice. "Even on the outside," I say as I set one glass in front of Dad, "they'll always be outsiders."

"Aren't you the devil's advocate!" Dad says with a grin. "Like mother, like daughter."

This is too much! "Dad! How can you talk so casually about Mom and get all excited about big changes in the world when *our* world is falling apart? Mom is gone!"

"What's wrong, Winnie? I thought talking to Mom today would cheer you up. She isn't gone for good. None of this is forever."

"So when is she coming back?"

"Well, I can't say precisely. There are a number of considerations ..."

"Dad! Can't you give me a straight answer for once?"

"Settle down here, Winnie, you're overreacting to—"

"Now I know exactly how Justice feels!"

"What *are* you talking about, Winnie?"

"Justice Goodwater! A few years ago his mother got dragged off to the state hospital here for no good reason, and now she's dead and buried without any explanation. He thinks maybe they kept her in a dungeon for some creepy experiments and she drowned trying to escape!"

"Listen, Winnie. I know there's a lot of speculation in the community about what goes on out here. It's true it isn't all pretty. Part of it stems from the history of this place. It started out as a debtor's prison, a place for derelicts of all sorts. Stories get exaggerated and passed down through families. You probably hear things at school. But try to remember that a lot of that talk is based on ignorance."

"Ignorance! Dad …"

"Look, Winnie, I know some things were done crudely in the past. Certain groups of patients have been used for testing new drugs and procedures for research, but it's not as sinister as it sounds. It's a way of acquiring valuable information for medical science."

"That doesn't make it right! They're not lab rats!" I say fiercely. The look on Dad's face tells me he's not convinced it's right either. "Dad, Justice doesn't even know which grave his mother is in! He deserves to be told that much! He's a person! And so am I! Nobody tells us—"

I've run out of air and words. Leaving Dad totally bewildered, I make a dash for my bedroom.

Soon I hear a gentle knocking on my door.

"What?" I snap.

"Your orange juice," Dad says. "I'll leave it out here for you, Winnie. And—ah—everything will be all right, honey. We'll figure things out. Good night."

27

My destination this afternoon is Watley Hall, the cottage where the babies and so-called babies live. I've been here before, on that first day when Dr. Bonner took Dad and me on a tour. Everything was a blur then, especially the big-headed babies, the *water-heads*. It felt wrong to be in the room, like gawking at an accident. Today, with my own nametag and the snack cart, I'm here on official business.

I'm doing my usual routine, talking to all the staff people and pointing out what's new on the cart. Then I see the name on the chart hanging on one of the cribs. *Timmy Tyler.* I peek around the bars.

"Hi! I'm Timmy." This sweet little voice comes from the mouth of a miniature face on a head big enough to wear a Hula-Hoop for a crown. "What's your name? Did you come to visit me?"

"I'm Winnie. I'm taking the snack cart around today."

Timmy lifts up a skinny, crooked arm and reaches through the crib bars to shake my hand. His fingers feel as fragile as bird bones.

"Your nametag says 'Winona.' Is Winnie your nickname, like Timmy is my nickname for Timothy?"

He reads! "Yes, that's right. I'm Winona May, Dr. May's daughter."

"I know Dr. May," Timmy says. "He's nice. I wish he'd come around every day, but the doctors have to take turns. Otherwise it wouldn't be fair."

"How old are you, Timmy?" I ask. He sounds so smart.

"Seventeen. I just had my birthday."

It seems impossible. This baby-sized boy in a crib would be a senior in high school if it weren't for that head.

"Hey there, chatterbox!" A woman wheeling a laundry cart has come up beside us. "Don't forget you promised to fold these towels for me."

"I'll do that," I say, reaching for a towel.

"Oh, no, thanks," the laundry lady says, setting a bundle to one side of Timmy's body. "This is one of Timmy's regular chores. You just watch and see what a good job he does."

I chat with Timmy while he pulls one towel at a time onto his stomach. He slides his crooked fingers along the hemmed edges and painstakingly matches up the corners of each bleached white towel. Little by little he creates a stack of neatly folded towels.

"How old are you, Winnie?" Timmy asks suddenly.

"Fourteen," I tell him.

"I have a sister the same age. She must be in the eighth grade now. Her name is Janet. Janet Elaine Tyler."

J.E.T. Mrs. Jetson. *Janet Tyler!*

28

A few months ago, I wouldn't have dreamed of inviting Janet Tyler to meet me at the soda fountain at Anderson's Drug Store. A few months ago, she wouldn't have been caught dead hanging out in public with the *girl from the nuthouse*. Today, here we are. But this Janet is different. Instead of trying to be the center of attention, she's trying to be invisible. Now I know why.

Having discovered Janet's secret makes me feel powerful. But what am I going to do with that power? That question makes my stomach do flip-flops. I take another bite of my butterscotch sundae to get up my courage.

"Remember when I had that stupid surprise party, Janet? And afterwards you asked about the guy who brought the food?"

Janet stops sucking her Green River, a swamp-colored drink made of one squirt of every flavor at the soda fountain. Her eyes lock onto mine. "Charlie. You said his name was Charlie. You said—"

"That's right, Mrs. Jetson, Janet Elaine Tyler." It makes me breathless to think I'm lifting the lid on this secret box Janet doesn't want to look into. "It was Charlie. But when you asked me about him, were you thinking his name might be, oh, Timmy, maybe?"

The color drains from Janet's face. Her hands fly up to her mouth, and she glances around at the other booths. Then she leans closer. "Have you told anyone else?"

"Not yet."

Janet squirms. "So what do you want?"

I had been hoping for friendship, actually, or at least a truce. But now that we're face to face, a dark current of revenge tugs at me. There's nothing I can do to strike back at the Starlings for ignoring me, nothing I can do to punish my parents for bringing me to this place, for lying to me and ruining my life. Now I have a chance to get even with Janet for treating me like a freak. It's my turn to show her what it feels like. My mind dances with the possibilities.

Janet's urgent whisper breaks into my thoughts. "What do I have to do to keep you from blabbing about my brother?"

Before I can come up with a response, I'm distracted by a group of girls settling into the next booth. One girl stumbles as she slides in. Dramatically, she flops down along the length of the seat with her head hanging over the end. Her friends laugh.

Suddenly in my mind I'm seeing Mary Ellen's head sticking out of a huge silver tube. The iron lung is as big as a Buick, with little porthole windows along the sides. A mirror is angled over Mary Ellen's face so at least she can make eye contact with the ghostly white masked and gowned people who enter her room. Including me. Any words we exchange have to be spoken between the rhythmic whooshes of the machine that keeps the air moving in and out of her lungs.

"Winnie, what are you staring at?" Janet's voice seems to be coming from a great distance.

The girl in the next booth has finished her clowning. She sits up and straightens her clothes. It's her sweater—baby-blue mohair—that catches my eye. It reminds me of one I used to have, my favorite, which I gave to Mary Ellen as a token of my phony friendship. I did it just to make myself feel better, but I ended up feeling worse. Mary Ellen liked it so much that she said she was going to be buried in it if she died.

"Winnie? Say something!"

"Mmm? What did you say?"

Janet is waiting. "Tell me, have you seen him?"

"Seen him?"

"Timmy! Have you actually seen him?"

"Oh! Um, yes. He says he wants to see you."

"He talks?"

"Well, sure, he talks." My control of this conversation is slipping away.

Janet keeps piling on questions like extra weight on her side of a teeter-totter. "He makes sense and everything?"

I nod. "He reads, too. He seems pretty smart."

"Oh, right! That's why he's there, because he's so smart!"

"Well, I think it's mostly his body that has the problem."

"So you told him about me?"

"No! He told me how much he's always wanted to meet his little sister, Janet, who's in the eighth grade. I figured that must be you."

By this time we're speaking so softly and leaning so far across the table that our noses are nearly touching. I see tears glistening in the corners of Janet's eyes. She pulls back and dabs at them with a napkin. "I don't know, Winnie. I just don't get it. My parents always told me Timmy was a vegetable. That's why they had to put him there. They said it would be better for all of us just to pretend he never existed, and then pretty soon—he wouldn't."

"He's not a vegetable."

"I've seen only one picture of Timmy," Janet says. "It was taken when he was about three. He was tied onto his tricycle. My mother said they did that because his big head kept tipping him over. But he was cute, in a way. He was smiling and—"

Janet stops and presses the heels of her hands against her leaky eyes.

"You could go and see him for yourself," I tell her.

"Go out there? Alone?" Janet gets a panicky look on her face.

"Uh, I don't know. Why would you have to go alone?"

"You'd go with me?"

"Me?"

"You're the one who knows your way around out there, Winnie."

"Oh, well, I don't—"

"Please, Winnie!"

The desperate look in her eyes is too much for me. "Okay, Janet. Okay."

I look away then. The tug of war inside me is over, at least for now.

29

It feels weird having Janet at my house. She seems nervous and keeps looking over her shoulder as if she's afraid someone might be sneaking up on her.

"I thought they'd give a doctor a fancier house than this," she says after I've shown her around and we're sitting on my bed. "My dad runs the woolen mill, and we have a bigger place than yours. With wall-to-wall carpeting."

"I know. Well, this is just temporary."

"Yeah, so you keep saying. Everything was bigger and better in Chicago. What's this?" Janet reaches over to pick up my snow globe.

"It's the place I used to live. I got that when I joined the Star—my group back home. We all went on a shopping trip together. Everybody got one."

Janet seems hypnotized by the swirling flakes. "Neat! Your own city under glass! Your own little life in a bubble!"

"Yeah, but it's starting to seem pretty far away."

Janet sets the globe back on the shelf, where a photo catches her eye. "So this must be your group, huh? Everybody's holding up a snow globe. Where are you?"

"Oh, I'm not in that one. I was taking the picture, as usual."

That's the bad part about being a photographer. You end up feeling like an outsider, like you were never part of what was going on around you. When you look back, there's no record that you were there at all.

Then Janet spies a photo of Mom and me wearing Mickey Mouse ears. "Hey, you've been to Disneyland?"

"Uh-huh. Last year. I know that's a goofy picture, but—"

"No," Janet says. "It's a Mickey picture."

"Ha-ha."

"Is this your mother? She looks so young! You look just alike. Especially the ears."

"Very funny. Maybe we should get going." I head toward the door.

Janet returns the photo to the shelf and plunks herself back on my bed. "After I found out about having an older brother out here, I thought maybe I was adopted, even though I know from pictures that I look a lot like my mother when she was young. Why would my parents risk having another baby of their own? Then I figured that if I was theirs I must have been an accident. A mistake. You know what I mean?" Janet gives me a meaningful look.

I nod.

"When I finally got up the nerve to ask my mom, she said I was a *surprise*. Timmy was the mistake. I wasn't sure if she meant hers and my father's, or God's."

I don't respond, so Janet goes on. "I suppose she said that to make me feel better, but it didn't. I hated knowing I really was related by blood to a retard who lives out—here." She pauses, fiddling with her hair. "I still do. If anybody at school found out—"

"Right. It's no fun to be treated like a zombie."

Janet looks away. "Sorry," she whispers.

"Well, at least it's not catching," I say. "Come on. Let's go meet your brother." I lead the way down the stairs.

"What—where are we going?" Janet asks in alarm. "My brother is in your basement?"

"You'll see."

As my hand closes around the key, I consider briefly whether this qualifies as an emergency. If we tried to walk in the front door of Timmy's building, we'd have to sign in and explain why we were there. Adults would be called—Janet's parents, Dad. *Then* we'd have an emergency.

We enter the tunnel.

Janet keeps freezing up and looking around so frantically that I'm afraid she'll turn back and run. The closer we get to Timmy's cottage, the more doubts I have. Maybe this whole thing is a mistake. What if the meeting is a disaster? Janet could make my life more miserable than ever.

"Um, Janet, there's something you should know before we get there."

"What?" I hear panic in Janet's voice. She stops abruptly. "Tell me!"

"Timmy thinks the reason he doesn't see you is that your family lives too far away to come for a visit. Maybe you should tell him you just moved here or something."

Janet looks at me like I'm from another planet. "Winnie, what's the point of me coming to meet Timmy if I'm just going to keep telling him lies?"

I shake my head, disgusted with myself. "Bad family habit," I mumble.

Janet marches ahead, ready to face what her parents have kept from her for so long.

As we approach Timmy's crib, I see that his eyes are closed. From the look on Janet's face I can tell that neither my words nor her own imagination has fully prepared her for the reality of this head—this monstrous, fluid-filled, blotchy-with-pressure-sores, bigger-than-a-beach-ball head that takes up half the crib—and the tiny bent body attached to it.

Janet stands mute and trembling as I say, "Hi, Timmy. I have a surprise for you."

His eyes flutter open.

"Your sister is here," I tell him.

"Hi, Timmy," Janet whispers.

"Janet Elaine Tyler? My sister?"

Janet nods and attempts a smile.

Timmy starts talking a mile a minute, telling Janet how pretty she is and how he's always dreamed of meeting her. Janet hesitates only a second before she takes his hand in both of hers. Pretty soon it's like they've forgotten I'm there. Tears are running down Janet's face.

Timmy calls her Little Sis and says, "Now that you've found your way, maybe it won't seem so far the next time you visit."

Watching Janet and Timmy together, I know at last that the only way to ease the pain of a secret is to face up to it and deal with it head on. It's time for me to write to Mary Ellen.

Back in my bedroom after Janet has left, I watch as a dying ray of late afternoon sunlight spreads a golden glow through my snow globe. I reach for my notebook.

Dear Mary Ellen,

> *Remember me? Winnie May—probably the last person on earth you expected to hear from. It's too bad we didn't get to spend much time together last year after you got out of the hospital, but I have been thinking a lot about you lately. My family moved to Minnesota a few months ago, but things just aren't working out here for me. Anyway, I'm wondering if you could do me a favor.*

No, that's no good. I rip the page out of my notebook and start over.

Dear Mary Ellen,

> *It's me, Winnie May. I should have done this a long time ago, but I'm writing now to say I'm sorry for the way things turned out last year when you got out of the hospital and came back to school. I didn't mean to be unfriendly; I just got so busy with everything else. I hope you understand. Anyway, as you probably know, I've been living in Minnesota for the past several months and all I can think about is getting back home to my real life and all my friends at Morningside.*

No, this one's worse! There's no way I can say *sorry* after all this time and ask for a favor in the very same letter. I tear the page to shreds.

Then I try to imagine what would happen if I managed to write the perfect letter and Mary Ellen said everything was okay between us and she invited me to stay with her. Living with Mary Ellen, how could I be a Starling? Is that what I even want anymore?

How did everything get so complicated? Why is it so hard to tell people how you feel and what you want?

There's only one letter I can write to Mary Ellen.

Dear Mary Ellen,
I'm sorry for the way I treated you—very, very sorry.
Winnie

I fold the page carefully and put it in an envelope. I stamp it and address it to Mary Ellen. Then I tuck the letter away in my underwear drawer, wondering what it counts for if I can't bring myself to mail it.

Nobody's coming to rescue me; I have to do it myself.

30

The clock says it's time to get ready for school, but it seems too dark. I peek outside and see that winter has arrived—in late April! The view from the living room picture window is Christmas-card calm. The newly budding trees and tiny blades of green grass, the roofs and sidewalks, are all blanketed in white. The birds, so noisy with their springtime activity just yesterday, are nowhere to be seen or heard.

I feel suddenly energized by this dramatic change, as if an inviting new backdrop has been plunked into my shipwrecked life, calling me to explore it, promising—something new! A temporary escape.

I hurry to dress and pull on boots I haven't needed to wear until now. I load my camera with fresh film and slip another roll into my pocket. I can't bear the thought of going to school today, so I move as quietly as possible, hoping to slip out before Dad wakes up. I leave a note for him on the kitchen table. *I had to leave early today.* Not the whole truth, but true enough. *See you later. Love, Winnie.*

I have one hand on the back door when I hear Dad's footsteps in the hall. Darn!

His voice stops me. "Wait, Winnie. Did you hear the news?"

"Hmm?" I pretend to be busy adjusting my scarf. "What news, Dad?" I've already decided that whatever it is, I'm not going to school.

"On the radio. They just announced that school is closed because of the snow."

I lift my eyes to his, to make sure he's not joking. "Really? No school?" I'm relieved not to have to sneak away after all. Then I remember my note. Dad follows my glance toward it on the kitchen table.

"Does that change your plans?" he asks.

"Um, not much," I admit.

Dad pulls the curtain aside to look out the kitchen window. His face is lit up with the same excitement I feel. "Lucky you!" he says.

Impulsively, I ask, "Can you come with me?"

He looks at the clock and shakes his head. "Have fun for both of us."

Overnight, snow has piled up in three-foot drifts, swirled by the wind into fantastic shapes. Our birdfeeder sports a towering top hat. The playhouse is frosted as perfectly as a wedding cake. Best of all are the trees with their branches furred like crystal caterpillars.

I imagine the kids in town putting aside the rules of cool on this unexpected holiday, stomping circles in the snow for games of fox and geese with younger brothers and sisters, building snowmen, racing down the Mill Hill on sleds, toboggans, and flying saucers.

I lurch and stagger through the snow. The exertion is thrilling, but I regret every footprint I leave in the perfect drifts, as if I've ruined an artist's fresh painting. But my tracks aren't the only thing changing the scenery. I'm in a race with the rising sun as it advances across the sky, unstoppable. Its rays are like burning wands touching each thickly coated branch in turn, releasing dazzling bursts of diamond dust.

I'm torn. I want to roll and tumble in the snow. I want to toss it and taste it and feel its stinging chill on my face. At the same time, I want to hold on to this scene at its peak of perfect beauty. The only way I can do that is with my camera, standing at a measured distance from it all. But even if my photos are good, they're only images, a representation, not the thing itself.

If Justice were here, my choice would be easy—we'd play the day away! I will him to appear, but he doesn't. I finish shooting my roll of film.

For a while longer I trudge around the hospital grounds like the last person on earth. Finally I end up in the playhouse, watching through the little window as icicles form and drop from the roof.

Another sparkling shower drifts down, another, and another. By mid-day the show is over. Once again the trees are a tangle of wet black bark, their branches like bare arms stretched to the sky, holding out for more.

31

By the time school would normally be ending, I feel restless. The day has been too long spent by myself. I've wasted the afternoon flipping through photo albums and watching soap operas. Finally it's three o'clock and I head for the door, eager to start my route with the snack cart.

I'm taken by surprise when I step outside and run into Janet. She looks red-cheeked and winded as she slogs her way up the sidewalk through the slushy remains of the snowstorm.

"Janet! What are you doing here?"

"I'm here to visit Timmy, of course," Janet says. "I told you yesterday I wanted to see him again soon. You're not leaving, are you?"

"Well, yes. I'm supposed to do my volunteer job today."

"But I'm freezing! I can't just turn around and walk all the way home again!"

"I never thought you'd come out here on a snow day, Janet. You should have called."

"Well, I'm here now," Janet says, stamping her feet. "Are you going to let me in or not?"

"Sure," I say, opening the front door for her. "You can wait inside till I get back."

"No! Please, Winnie, just this once more."

I've told Janet I can't keep sneaking her in from my house through the tunnels. She has to get her parents to bring her to visit Timmy through the front door of his cottage.

"Janet! I'm nearly late already!"

"So what? It's not like a real job. Please, Winnie!"

"All right, all right. I'll take you there, but we'll go to the canteen and pick up the snack cart first. Hurry up."

"Thanks, Winnie."

We throw off our coats and scarves in my bedroom and pound down the basement stairs. For the third time I unlock the forbidden door.

We've gone only a short distance into the tunnel when I realize I've left my nametag and whistle in the pocket of my coat. It may not be a big deal; I'll probably be allowed to take the cart anyway. But I'm tired of being pushed around by Janet.

"Listen, Janet. I need you to help me out." I press the key into her hand. "You run back upstairs to my bedroom and get my nametag and whistle from my coat pocket. I'll go pick up the cart. We'll meet back here in about ten minutes. Then we'll go straight to Timmy."

"No! Don't leave me down here by myself, Winnie!"

"It's only one left turn to get back to my house, Janet. You'll be fine. And on the way back here, you'll have the whistle. In case …"

"In case what?"

"In case you need it."

I sprint away into the tunnel before Janet has time to refuse.

It takes me longer than the ten minutes I promised Janet to return with the cart. Before I reach our meeting place, I hear the shrill blasts of a whistle echoing through the maze of passageways ahead of me. A pit opens in my stomach. I leave the cart and race ahead.

"Janet!" I scream at each intersection. "Janet! Where are you?"

I turn right and left, trying to locate the place the sound is coming from.

"W-W-W-Winnie!" I hear at last. "W-W-W-Winnie!"

I find Janet, wild-eyed and panting with fear. She sits crouched with her back pressed against the wall. My whistle lies on the floor beside her. A short distance from her sits Charlie, rocking hard. Red scratches crisscross his face and forearms.

"Janet! What happened? Are you okay?" I reach out to touch her, but she slaps my hand away. Even though it must be eighty degrees in here, Janet is shaking like we're trapped in a freezer.

"Get me out of here! I should never have trusted you, acting so friendly all of a sudden! You did this on purpose!"

"No, of course I didn't, Janet!" I turn to Charlie. "What happened here, Charlie? Tell me what happened!"

"Ch-Charlie wants to help. Okay? G-Girl is l-l-lost. Charlie knows t-tunnels. Ch-Ch—"

"He tried to drag me off and—"

"No, Janet! Charlie wouldn't—"

"The other one! He had those big dirty paws all over me! Then this one came along—"

"Ch-Charlie wants to help. Okay? Tell V-Vince d-don't hurt her! Wh-Why g-girl is m-mad at Ch-Charlie?"

I bury my face in my hands. I want all this to go away. I drop down between Janet and Charlie. I pick up the whistle and blow, over and over, until help arrives.

Dad is so upset by what happened with Janet, Vince, and Charlie that he won't even listen to my side of the story.

"What were you thinking, leaving her down there alone?" he demands for about the hundredth time, without giving me a chance to answer. "You put Janet and yourself in a dangerous situation today, Winnie. I thought you were mature enough to use better judgment. How could you pull a prank like that?"

Prank! How can he think I was pulling a prank? I keep trying to make things better and they just get worse! I wish Mom were here to tone Dad down. All I can do is sit on my bed and grind my teeth, waiting for Dad to leave the room so I can scream into my pillow.

But Dad goes on and on. "This is precisely the sort of thing that makes the institution look bad in the eyes of the community. It gives the whole state hospital system a bad name. And what about my position here? I can't afford any more trouble!"

"What will happen to Charlie? And Vince?"

Dad stops pacing to stare out the window. He shakes his head. "Vince will be sent to a more secure facility, I'm sure. Probably for good this time. Charlie, I don't know. Certainly he'll be more restricted for a while."

"I'm sorry," I whisper.

"Sorry isn't enough, Winnie. You're nearly an adult! When you make a conscious decision to break the rules, even if you think it's for a good reason, you have to accept the consequences." He gets a funny look on his face when he says this and shakes his head, as if he's trying to chase away annoying thoughts.

"What consequences?" I manage to ask.

He waves my question off. "We'll talk about this later, Winnie. We *both* have a lot to think about." He closes my bedroom door behind him and leaves me to my pillow.

32

After waiting more than two hours for Dad to decide on my consequences, I make a plan of my own. I open my bedroom door quietly and see that he is absorbed in watching *Gunsmoke*. Then I slip out of my room to the telephone in the hall. The cord is just long enough to stretch into the front coat closet. I close the door as tightly as I can and sit among the boots and overcoats, waiting for my eyes to adjust to the darkness.

Every time I pick up the receiver, my breath starts coming too fast. I don't know exactly what I'm going to say. I only hope Pam will sound the same as she used to—giggly and a little sassy-mouthed. I still haven't figured out exactly what her letter meant.

Finally, I just do it. *Outside line, please. Long-distance.* The phone rings, once, twice.

"Hello, Winstads' residence." A male voice. Pam's older brother? Her father?

"Hi, um—is Pam there?" I shift uncomfortably at the dopey sound of my own voice, setting off a jangle of wire hangers above me.

"Who's calling, please?"

"Winnie," I squeak.

"Who?"

"Winnie May."

A pause. "Okay. Hold on."

I hold on for what seems like a long time, trying to make sense of the muffled sounds on the other end. Finally, "Hello." No giggles, no sass.

I try to make up for the flatness in Pam's voice with extra enthusiasm in my own. "Pam! It's me, Winnie! Calling from Never-Never Land! Life is so insane ..." No—I don't want to talk about my life here. I start again. "Um, it's been ages! How are you—and all the others?"

"Fine."

"Oh, well—good. That's great! It's just so good to hear your voice!"

"Yeah, well, why are you calling me, Winnie? What do you want?"

"What do I want? Well, I want to come back, of course, and I need to make plans. Like I said in my letter. Well, that was a long time ago now. Did you share it with the other Starlings? I wrote to them, too. What does everybody think?"

"About what?"

This isn't going well. Maybe I've caught Pam at a bad time. Maybe she's in the middle of one of her famous arguments with her mother. "Maybe I should call back later, Pam, if this—"

"No! Don't call back. Just tell me what you want. If it's your Fabian records ..."

"Pam, I don't care about the records. Listen, things are really bad here right now. Can't I come and stay with you, just to finish the school year? There's only about a month left now. Please? I have to get away …" My throat is closing up. I can't believe I'm begging!

"No, Winnie! Don't you get it? You can't just come back and expect everybody to pretend nothing happened!"

"What, Pam? What happened?"

"Oh, stop acting so innocent! That whole scandal with your father! That's what!"

"Scandal?"

"Everybody says he got off easy. He's lucky he didn't go to jail!"

"Jail! Pam, I didn't think—"

"No, Winnie, I guess you didn't. How can you imagine that you could ever be a Starling with a father who belongs in jail?"

"But, Pam, I didn't do—"

"Listen, Winnie, it's not like we hate you or anything. We know you can't help what your parents do, but—we have all the Starlings we need. Jamie Naughton took your place."

"Jamie?"

"Remember her? That really tall girl in our class, the one who was in an ad for Marshall Field's last year? She's a real model and a super dancer, so we've all bought red patent-leather tap shoes, and—"

I replace the receiver and push the closet door open a crack. *Gunsmoke* is still blazing. Dad doesn't hear me when I set the telephone back on the hall table. He doesn't hear me tiptoe into my room and close the door.

I pick up my snow globe and hold it with both hands as I step up onto the bed, bouncing a little to set the stars in motion. I take one last look at the sparkling little fake world in a bubble, the world I wanted for so long to shrink myself back into, and then I send it on a fast flight across the room. It hits the wall and explodes in a glittering shower of glass, water, and snow stars. Free from their confinement, the silver stars look more beautiful than ever. The space around them sets each one apart as they spread out like a glittering net and settle onto the floor.

Dad comes running. "Winnie! What happened? Are you all right?"

"Don't come in here, Dad!" I warn him as soon as the door swings open. "Broken glass."

He takes in the scene and remains on the other side of the threshold. "What a mess! You're sure you're not hurt?"

"It *is* a mess, isn't it? Everything's a mess." I remain standing on my bed and continue to bounce slightly, enjoying this perspective, looking down on Dad. My heart is wide open, wounded but ready for anything. It doesn't matter what happens next. I feel bold and reckless.

"I'll get a mop and some—"

"No, Dad, wait! What happened in Chicago? Tell me what you did!"

"Winnie, honey," Dad says, wiggling his stockinged toes on the other side on the debris between us. "What brought this on?"

"I called Pam Winstad. She told me everybody thinks you belong in jail. You did something that's wrecked my life and you don't explain anything! I deserve to know, Dad!"

"Okay, Winnie, okay."

Dad remains standing in the hall, his head hung low, breathing deeply for a few minutes, like he's gathering his thoughts. Finally he clears his throat.

"I broke some rules, Winnie. We all did. All the doctors in my group."

"What kind of rules?"

"Abortion rules."

"Abortion! Dad!"

"Listen to me now, Winnie. In most states it's almost impossible for a woman to end a pregnancy unless it threatens her own life. But in a few states, Illinois among them, the law recognizes other reasons that might make abortion the best choice."

"Like what? What makes killing unborn babies a good choice?"

"I didn't say it was ever a good choice, Winnie. In some situations there simply are no good choices."

That's something I understand. I wait for Dad to say more.

"For instance, Winnie, if we have some indication that the baby might be abnormal."

I think of Timmy. Would he be better off if he hadn't been born? "So you think only perfect babies have a right to live?"

"No, Winnie, I'm not saying that. But I can understand that a woman might think twice about giving birth to a baby she knows is likely to spend its entire life in an institution."

"But Dad—"

"There are other considerations, too. What if a woman is raped and becomes pregnant? Should she be forced to have that baby? What if she's still a young girl herself? Like Janet. Think what could have happened to Janet."

What happened to Janet was bad enough; I never thought about how much worse it could have been. I feel like I'm being pulled off-track. "Dad, I just want to know why. Why did you—?"

"Okay, Winnie," Dad says, running a hand through his hair. "I understand. But *you* have to understand how complicated these decisions are for doctors. We take an oath to do no harm, but sometimes it comes down to doing the least harm. Women travel from all across the country to see doctors in Chicago and New York and California, hoping to get the legal abortion they can't get at home. Some have good reasons, some don't. If we refuse them, well, we know most of them will get an abortion anyway, an illegal one done by someone who isn't qualified. Sometimes it costs these women—and girls—their lives."

"So what happened, Dad? Tell me!"

"All the doctors in my practice were providing this service. Too freely, in my opinion. We got a reputation for doing abortions on demand, no questions asked. I couldn't control what the other men were doing, but when a woman came to me, especially a well-to-do woman, who was obviously thinking simply of how inconvenient it would be to have a child, I refused to help her. In some cases I referred women like that to one of the other physicians in the group, but in this one case, I flat-out refused and sent her away."

"So?"

"Well, she got her abortion anyway, of course. But she was so angry that she blew the whistle on me."

"But you didn't do the abortion."

"Not for her. But she knew of others who had gotten an abortion from me."

"Did you know at the time you were breaking the law?"

"Winnie, I thought the law was too strict, and I thought my partners were too lenient. I honestly believed my approach was the most reasonable one."

"But you knew it was against the law?"

"Maybe it's a tendency of those of us in the medical profession to think we're the exception to the high and holy rules we hold everyone else to."

"Dad!"

This time he looks me straight in the eye. "Yes, Winnie. I knew."

Dad's answer lands like a blow. Pam was telling the truth. There has to be more to the story, though. "Why didn't all the doctors get in trouble?" I ask Dad.

"Well, Winnie, that part may be even harder to understand. As the newest partner in the group, the one who had caused the trouble, I was the one who had to take the blame."

"But that's not fair! Why didn't you tell on the others?"

"It could have made things worse, Winnie, for everybody. All the other doctors had their high-powered lawyers making deals, and this is what they offered me: If I'd take the whole blame, without pointing a finger at my partners, I'd receive a lighter punishment. Five years' suspension from private medical practice. Otherwise, we'd all probably have lost our licenses for good. And possibly gone to jail."

"It's still not fair."

"That's what your mother said, too. She wanted me to fight. But the thought of going to court over this—I just couldn't face all that. Probably I was too willing to take the easy way out. I'm the one who wasn't being fair. To any of us."

"Did you and Mom think you could keep this secret from me forever? Did you think I'd never find out? And that would make it all okay?"

"I didn't want to hurt you, Winnie."

I can't listen to any more of this. "Please just leave me alone, Dad," I tell him. And he does.

33

Dad is in the shower and I'm lying in bed wondering if he even knows this is Mother's Day. I wonder if Mom knows. She hasn't been acting much like a mother lately. I thought about sending her a card. I even bought one. It said: *Home is where your Mom is.* I wanted to add *supposed to be,* just to make her feel guilty. Instead I wrote, *Missing you, Winnie,* and stuffed the card in my underwear drawer next to the letter I wrote to Mary Ellen.

I've almost drifted back to sleep when the doorbell rings, setting off alarms inside me. Who'd be coming to our house at this hour on a Sunday morning? I throw off the covers and hurry to the door, expecting trouble.

Here it is, standing on its two hind legs. "Smokey! What are you doing here?"

The clever creature strikes the doorbell with his front hooves again. "Bleah!" he pleads, as if to ask if I can come out and play. When I reach out to stroke his head, he dodges and tries to sneak past me into the house.

"No, Smokey! Stop!" We wrestle for a few minutes on the rug in the front hall in a tangle of shoes and scarves. Finally I manage to shove him out and slam the door. "Ooof! You silly beast!"

The bell sounds again. I know I'll have to go out there and

somehow drag him back to the farm. I pull on my jacket and slip out the back door, leash in hand. I peek around the corner of the house. He's still standing on the front steps, battering the bell and bleating for attention. My heart softens a little.

"Hi, Smokey-boy," I croon. "Come over here now. Come on, boy."

Smokey's head swings in my direction. He cocks his head and waits for my next move. I take a step toward him. As if that's the starting signal to a race, Smokey is off and running.

Instantly, I'm back on boil. "Smokey! Come back here, you little devil!"

"Off on another wild goat chase?" says a familiar voice.

"Justice! What are you doing here?"

"You probably won't believe it, but I'm here to see your father."

"My father! What for?"

"To thank him. I'll just be a minute. Then I'll help you round up Smokey."

"Oh, I see," I say, even though I don't. "Well, okay." I invite Justice to come inside, and for the first time, he follows me into the house.

By this time Dad is dressed and sitting at the kitchen table with the morning paper. "Dad, Justice is here to see you." I practically hold my breath trying to anticipate Dad's reaction to seeing Justice here face to face.

Dad stands and extends a hand to Justice. "Good morning, young man."

Justice glances at his own hands nervously before accepting Dad's. I stand close to Justice, feeling protective. And curious. "I'm sorry to bother you, Dr. May, I just wanted—"

"It's no bother. Have a seat," Dad says, indicating a chair.

"No, thanks," Justice says, his eyes darting around the room. "I won't stay long. I just came to thank you for what you did. My grandmother thanks you, too."

"You're welcome, Justice. Both of you. It wasn't very difficult to get the information. You should have been told in the first place."

"What did you do, Dad? What's going on?"

Justice looks impatient with me. "Winona! It's about my mother. You know. Her grave. It's number 138."

"Oh. But what does that have to do with—how did you find that out?"

"Your father, Winona. He got the hospital to send an official letter to us. We were wrong about the drowning part; she died of pneumonia. We got an apology from Dr. Bonner."

Even the good news Dad keeps secret! I'm furious and thrilled at the same time and have no words at all.

"It's just the beginning," Dad says to Justice. "Letters will be sent to all the families with relatives in the cemetery. You know, I was in the dark about this until Winnie brought it to my attention. I've contacted the governor about looking into the situation at other institutions around the state, too. The system is deeply flawed. But it's a start."

Justice nods and lets out a sigh. He looks relieved. "Well, thanks again, Dr. May. Um, I should go now."

"Wait a moment," Dad says, reaching out to touch Justice lightly on the shoulder. "I—um—just wanted to say, well, this has been a difficult year for our family, and—uh—I haven't always—

that is, Winnie has—"

The sound of the doorbell makes us all jump.

Expecting Smokey, I yank open the door, prepared to make a tackle. "Mom!"

Dad pulls her into the house and I close the door quickly behind her, as if we're afraid she might fly away again. I can't decide if I want to leap into her arms and bury my face against her shoulder or start scolding her. I feel shaky with the effort of holding back all my mixed-up feelings.

The tension in the room makes Justice uncomfortable. He greets Mom briefly, and then he offers to go after Smokey. Before he leaves he looks hard at me, as if he wants to say something. After a moment he drops his eyes and slips away.

34

Mom and Dad and I sit at the kitchen table in awkward silence for a moment. "Isn't anyone going to wish me a happy Mother's Day?" Mom asks. She flicks her eyes back and forth between Dad and me and fiddles nervously with her rings.

Dad reaches across the table and takes Mom's hands in his. He pulls in a trembling breath and nods but keeps his lips pressed together.

I'm caught again in a tug-of-war going on inside me, like the time when Janet and I met at the soda fountain. This time I give in to the surge of spite washing over me. "What exactly are you doing here, Mom? Are you passing through on a little visit? Did you come back just to collect bouquets for being such a great mother?"

"Oh, no, honey, I—"

"Winnie, don't talk to your mother like that!" Dad breaks in.

"I *will* talk like this!" I strike the table with my palms. "To both of you! And I want you to talk to me! I feel so alone here!"

"Please, Winnie, we don't—" Mom starts to say.

"You pull me away from my friends and my school without telling me why. You tell me not to talk about family matters because it's nobody's business, but family matters are my business! You treat me like an outsider in my own family!"

"What?" Mom says.

"Winnie!" Dad says.

"You don't give me credit for having any judgment at all! It was bad enough to finally find out, after everybody else back home already knew, that Dad nearly went to jail for doing abortions! And Mom cracked up and abandoned me! Now Dad is making plans to leave, and I suppose you're getting a divorce, so I'll probably wind up in Cottage 14! I'm hardly going to blab all that for Show-and-Tell!"

For a second my parents' mouths hang open in silence. Then they look at each other and burst out laughing.

I'm so shocked at their response that I push myself away from the table and bolt out the back door. I hear the two of them coming after me as I run across the backyard, down the slope, behind the stand of pine trees, and right into the playhouse.

I slam the little door in their faces. "Leave me alone!" There's no lock on the door, so I scramble up the ladder to the loft and sit on the trap door. Through a crack I can see the two of them crouched below me. For a long time nobody speaks.

"Winnie," Mom says at last. "Please listen."

"I don't like to be laughed at and I don't want to hear any more phony excuses!"

"No excuses, Winnie. Just an explanation. I left because I didn't think you or Dad needed me the way I was. I felt so useless. I figured you'd be better off without me for a while. I'd sunk into such a dark fog of my own that I couldn't see how troubled you were. I know Dad has talked to you about everything that happened with his medical practice back in Chicago. We've agreed it was a mistake not to tell you sooner, and we're sorry that—"

"I've heard all this! You thought I was too young, right? That I didn't need to know?"

"Winnie," Mom says, "we were trying to protect you."

"From the truth?"

"Yes!" Mom says, surprising me. "From the hard truth of growing up."

I open the trap door and peer down at my parents.

"When you were a little girl," Dad says, "your mother and I thought we could protect you from everything. We wanted to give you a life that was happy and easy. I suppose it wasn't realistic to think we could keep it that way forever; it just ended more abruptly than we expected. And I never imagined I'd be shielding you from my own misdeeds …" Dad's voice trails off and he sits there shaking his head. "The world is so much more complicated than we ever imagine when we're young and full of high ideals."

"Stop torturing yourself, Max," Mom says, running a hand over his forehead. "We all have things we're not proud of. It isn't the misdeeds as much as denying them, covering them up. Eventually they start to fester. Do you understand that, Winnie?"

"Um—yeah." I'm thinking of Mary Ellen, of course, so who am I to judge Dad? The rage is beginning to drain out of me; plain old sadness is taking its place. The world *is* much more complicated than I imagined.

"Let's make a new pact here," Mom says. "In our defense, your father and I aren't mind readers. So, in the future, ask. If you ask, we'll tell."

"The whole story," I say. "Otherwise I have to fill in the blanks for myself, and—"

"And as we've noticed," Dad says, "you have a vivid imagination. So, yes—the whole story."

"Even if it isn't pretty," Mom adds. "Anything else, Winona?"

"Yes." My name. Suddenly it seems important to know. "How did you choose my name, Mom?"

"Your name? Well, Winona, years ago, fifteen to be exact, your dad and I got stranded in a sweet little river town by that name. We got a room in a small inn and stayed up all night watching the lightning over the bluffs."

From the look my parents exchange I can tell they're back in that place now.

"It was a very romantic evening in Winona," Dad says. "We wanted to remember it forever."

It embarrasses me to hear this from my parents, but I like knowing that my life started as a plan instead of an accident or a mistake. Still, I have another, more difficult question. I clear my throat. "Are you back to stay, Mom, or are you two splitting up?"

"Not splitting up," Mom says. "But I am going back to Pennsylvania."

My stomach takes a plunge.

"We all are," Dad says. "Thanks to connections I've made with a couple of old doctor pals in the past few months, I've been offered a position in the state hospital system at an institution near Philadelphia. My job won't be much different there, but we won't have to live on the grounds. And the local school is sure to be bigger."

"We're really leaving Bridgewater?"

"It won't be like our life in Chicago," Mom says quietly, "but I think we'll all be happier than we have been for a while."

My head is spinning with all this. I don't have the dancing-on-the-moon feeling I expected if this wish ever came true. And I don't know yet how I feel about Dad, knowing he did those abortions. I guess as long as we can keep talking, keep things out in the open between us, I'll be all right. The tight knot inside me has finally begun to loosen.

I climb down from the loft, and one by one we duck our heads as we leave the playhouse. While Dad gets busy making coffee, I sneak off to my room to get that Mother's Day card. I promise myself to put the letter to Mary Ellen in the mail, too.

Watching Mom open her card, while Dad sizzles up some breakfast for us, I decide my parents aren't communist spies or liars after all, just regular people wandering in the dark passageways, making sense of what they can and letting the rest go.

35

It's the last day of school. Lunch will be served picnic-style today, and there will be relay races afterwards, so the dress code is casual. Most of the boys have on blue jeans and tennis shoes. Many of the girls are wearing pedal pushers or Bermuda shorts.

Before Mrs. Ames quiets the class so she can take attendance for the last time, Janet turns to face me. We haven't spoken much since the tunnel episode. "So you really are leaving this time, New Girl?"

I smile. "Yes, I really am leaving. Next week at this time I'll be in King of Prussia."

"That sounds like someplace you'd live," she says. "What country is that in, anyway?"

"It's not that exotic, just a suburb of Philadelphia. It's not at all like Chicago, but it's close to my mom's family, so I'll get to see my cousins. I've been there a few times before, so it won't be like moving someplace totally new."

"Or totally weird, you mean. Like Bridgewater."

I make a face at this. "Dad will still be working at a mental hospital, so I'll feel right at home."

"Indubitably!"

"Class!" Mrs. Ames says. "Please quiet down now, people! I

know it's the last day of school, but that means school is still in session. If we don't get started with our recitations, we'll be here all summer. And we'll never get to our popcorn."

That gets everyone's attention. Poetry and popcorn is the end-of-the-year tradition here. Beginning with Patsy Anderson, clear on through to Bruce Zimke, we take our turns sharing the poems we've memorized.

My stomach is full of butterflies as I walk to the front of the room to take my turn. I'm not worried about forgetting the words, just a little nervous about revealing thoughts that feel so personal. It's amazing that some guy who lived halfway around the world a hundred and fifty years ago could create a poem that feels like it was written just for me. I sweep the room with my eyes and begin: "'The Prisoner of Chillon,' by George Gordon, Lord Byron.

"There were in a dungeon cast,
Of whom this wreck is left the last …

"It was at last the same to me
Fettered or fetterless to be …

"These heavy chains to me have grown
A hermitage—and all my own!
And half I felt as they were come
To tear me from a second home …

"My very chains and I grew friends,
So much a long communion tends
To make us what we are:—even I
Regained my freedom with a sigh."

Off to my right, I hear a whisper. "Will you write to me, Winnie?" From the left, "Me, too?" A note is passed, and another. Addresses. I swallow hard and nod. Yes. Yes.

36

At Cottage 14 I sign Rose out and get her settled in the wagon. Justice is waiting for us. The sky is high and clear; a thrilling, gusty breeze sets the greening branches of the big elms dancing above us. Like a sunflower, Rose turns her face to the source of all that light and heat.

"You'll take her out when I'm gone, won't you?" I ask Justice.

"Sure," he says. "Both Smokey and Rose. If Rose is willing to have me without you."

I unzip my plaid flannel-lined jacket, pull my arms from the sleeves, and hand it to Justice. "If you wear this, maybe she'll feel more comfortable at first."

Justice holds the jacket to his face and inhales deeply. He takes off the corduroy shirt he's wearing over a T-shirt and pulls on my jacket. "This is yours," he says, giving me the corduroy shirt. "If you want it."

Now it's my turn. I inhale the sweet scent of Justice and then put on the shirt. For one last time together we head for the Mill Hill. Already it feels like we're saying goodbye.

After we've walked in silence for a few blocks, Justice says, "I thought you'd bring your camera. Did you forget it?"

I shake my head. I've decided that life—the weird, the wicked, and the wonderful parts of it—don't have to be captured on film or paper. Maybe not even spoken. Just experienced, right here, right now, while we have it.

By the time we arrive, Rose is rocking with impatience. From the top of the hill we look out over the Spirit River. The leaves of the cottonwoods along its banks aren't yet big enough to conceal the meandering path the water determines for itself.

"Oh! Oh! Oh!" Rose insists, eager to get on with it.

I climb into the wagon in front of her, tucking my legs beneath me. Rose slides her arms around my middle.

Justice eyes the terrain ahead of us and lines up the wagon. He unties the rope from the front and places the steering handles in my grip. "Remember," he says, "don't fight the bumps; let them launch you."

I take a deep breath and shiver with a surge of anticipation.

"Ready to fly?" he asks.

Then we do something crazy: we kiss! At the same instant and perfectly on target—as if we did this all the time—our lips meet, then part, like a bird making a brief touchdown on the water before lifting and soaring back into the air.

Without lingering, Justice moves behind the wagon and gives us a great running push, speeding us headlong down the beckoning slope.

I feel Rose's arms tighten around me. "Hold on tight, my little Rosey-Posey," I say. "This time we'll hit the bumps just right!"